I0780952

Cozy Up
to Mystery

a novel about bookworms,
a cat, love, and murder

by Colin Conway

Cozy Up to Mystery

Copyright © 2024 Colin Conway

ISBN: 978-1-961030-27-5

Cover design by Zach McCain

Original Ink Press, an imprint of High Speed Creative, LLC
1521 N. Argonne Road, #C-205
Spokane Valley, WA 99212

Visit the author's website at colinconway.com.

For the Book Dragons

"It's been a long time since I burst into
tears because a policeman didn't like me."

- Dashiell Hammett, *The Maltese Falcon*

Cozy Up
to Mystery

Chapter 1

Asher Reed strode through the main lobby, his shiny shoes landed heavily on the tile floor. The inside of his forearm brushed the little radio clipped to his belt. Overhead, a crooner belted out "That's Life" from hidden speakers. Ash adjusted his course to the reception desk by giving a wide berth to the hotel's fountain, an oddly prominent feature for this establishment.

In the center of the fountain stood a glazed ceramic baby with wings, a trumpet pressed against his lips. Chlorine-treated water sputtered from the instrument's bell, creating an uneven pitter-patter as droplets hit the pool below. The whole setup gave the unintended impression the cherub was blowing drool.

The fountain had the regrettable ability to attract unsupervised children. Five stood around the feature now, splashing their hands on top of the water and gleefully babbling some adolescent nonsense. Ash usually ignored all kids, a practice he found essential for a happy life. Today was no different, thus he widened his path to avoid them.

In front of the reception desk, a short woman in blue polyester slacks and a bright yellow T-shirt waited. Her silver hair was cut short in an almost military manner. A large red suitcase stood near her leg. Four bungee cords crisscrossed the bag, two along its width, the others encompassed its height.

Behind the registering woman, a line of impatient guests waited. They were dressed in various forms of attire. Several wore T-shirts, many wore jeans, and a couple wore polyester slacks. The majority were women and all but one carried an expression of frustration.

An attractive woman in her late-thirties wore a tight red dress that hugged every curve before stopping mid-thigh. Long blond hair fell to the middle of her back. She spun a large antique magnifying glass in her hand while a bulky art portfolio bag was slung over her shoulder. The woman waved discreetly toward the hotel's concierge, and he politely returned the gesture.

The desk clerk glanced at Ash, then shifted his attention to his computer. Finley Hester was a slender white man, prone to twitching and nervous giggles. Ash learned this about the clerk while working the past six weeks at Coastal Haven, the most prominent hotel in Marlowe Bay. The small city on the Georgia coast was an hour drive south of Savannah and about the same distance north of Jacksonville, Florida. Guests on the hotel's east side were treated to a view of the Atlantic Ocean, which was just across the boardwalk.

Finley cleared his throat. "I'm sorry, ma'am. I don't see a registration."

"It's gotta be in there." The woman in the bright yellow shirt put her hands on the counter and stood on her tiptoes to better see the clerk's computer. "Estelle," she said. "Estelle Enderby." She spelled out her last name. "I've been here many times."

"I can see you've been a guest previously, however, there's no active reservation." Finley motioned helplessly toward the computer. "I'm sorry, ma'am," he said once again, this time with a panicky chuckle.

"Not sure why you find this funny." Estelle dropped to her normal height, her chin barely above the counter. She noticed Ash and stepped back, revealing the words splashed across her shirt—*Mystery Mavens*. "You must be the muscle."

Ash ran his hand down his burgundy vest, smoothing it in place. He thought it made a striking statement along with his black slacks and black long-sleeved shirt. "I'm the porter." Ash reached for her suitcase.

"Nope." Estelle rolled her bag closer, clutching its handle with both hands. "You don't look like any bellhop I've ever seen." She considered the ball of fire tattooed on the back of Ash's hand. "Work release?"

"Ma'am?" Ash asked.

Finley cleared his throat again and followed it with an anxious cough. "We do have one room available, Ms. Enderby."

Estelle abruptly turned to the clerk. Her hands remained clutched on the suitcase handle, causing it to swirl around her and bang noisily onto the counter. "I'll take it."

"It's a double."

"I said I'd take it, and don't even think about up-charging me because of the second bed."

"No, ma'am." Finley squeaked, froze momentarily at the sound, then laughed self-consciously. "Don't know what that was."

Estelle cast a suspicious glance at Ash. "Still here?"

"It's my job," he said.

"Not with my bag."

Several other guests joined the registration line. A tall, older woman stood at the rear. She wore a yellow T-shirt like Estelle's, but her silver hair fell to her shoulders.

"It's the last available room in the whole hotel," Finley announced, obviously pleased by this discovery. He tapped a button with unnecessary flair. "Today is your lucky day."

"If I was lucky," Estelle said with narrowing eyes, "you wouldn't have lost my reservation."

"Right. Totally right." His gaze lowered to her driver's license, which sat next to his keyboard. "Still in California? How's the weather this time of year?"

"Enough chitchat." Estelle impatiently tapped the counter. "Just get me that room. I caught the red eye to get here on time, so I don't have the energy to deal with this nonsense."

"Yes, ma'am." The desk clerk now worked the keyboard with controlled enthusiasm.

Estelle looked over her shoulder at the tall woman in the matching T-shirt at the back of the line. "What took you so long?" she hollered.

"I stopped to talk with—"

"Never mind that." Estelle held up a hand, cutting off her friend. "They don't have my registration."

"What about mine?" the woman called across the lobby.

"Let me check." Estelle looked at the clerk. "What about Maxine's?"

"Who?"

"Maxine Coleman." She thumbed over her shoulder. "My friend."

Finley smiled at Maxine, then turned back to Estelle. "I'll verify her registration as soon as we're done."

"If you got hers and not mine, we're gonna have some trouble."

"Yes, ma'am. Of course."

Estelle glanced over her shoulder at the growing line of guests waiting to check in. She waved at the woman in the tight red dress who playfully looked back through her square head magnifying glass. Estelle smiled, then faced Finley again. "You need more help."

The desk clerk's nervous laugh worsened. It came out in staccato bursts, like giggling gunfire. *Ha. Haha. Ha.* Beads of sweat formed on the clerk's forehead. "We've had an outbreak."

"*Outbreak?*"

The guests standing immediately behind Estelle echoed her one-word question.

Finley grimaced, then smiled apologetically toward the waiting line. "The flu. It's fine to stay here. Perfectly fine, I promise." He looked at Estelle. "We sent the affected employees home yesterday."

"What about the manager?"

"She's sick, too," the desk clerk said.

"Who's in charge?"

Finley stopped typing. "I guess I am."

"Lord help us," Estelle muttered. She gestured toward Ash. "What about this one? Can't he help with the computers?"

"He's a porter, ma'am."

"So he said." She studied Ash. "You look familiar. Where do I know you from?"

"I have one of those faces," Ash said.

"No, you don't." Estelle waggled her finger. "I swear I've seen you somewhere. Maybe the post office wall?"

"They don't do that anymore," Ash said.

"You answered that quickly. Ever done any modeling?" Something occurred to Estelle, and she spun toward Finley. She impatiently pointed over the counter at his computer. "Don't forget my discount."

The desk clerk lifted his hands from the keyboard. "Discount?"

"For the conference." She pulled at the edges of her shirt to highlight its text. "We're here for Mystery Readers of America, only the best biblio-event in the entire world."

"Yes, of course." Finley cleared his throat. "Unfortunately—"

"No," Estelle said. "Don't say it."

"—I can't give you the room discount."

"You will. You can bet your bippy on that."

"I'm sorry, ma'am. We give those concessions to early registrants."

"You owe me the discount." Estelle stood on her tiptoes again and glared at Finley. "I registered long before the deadline."

"Well," the desk clerk said, now waving helplessly at the monitor. "The computer says otherwise."

Estelle's face widened with anger. She huffed once, then shook her head in disbelief. "You think I'm lying?"

Finley sputtered, "I'm just saying—"

"The computer is not always right." Estelle dropped onto her heels and glanced back. She motioned toward her friend. "Maxie! Come up here. This joker thinks I'm lying! He's not giving me the discount!"

The other waiting guests oohed as they turned to Estelle's friend.

Finley raised his hands in surrender. "I said nothing of the sort." He looked down at Estelle. "Please, tell them I didn't say you were lying."

Maxine dragged a blue suitcase behind her as she hurried to meet her friend. The plastic wheels clacked across the floor tiles. Maxine waved and smiled at the woman in the red dress as she passed. When she arrived at the front desk, Maxine asked Estelle, "Isn't it great that Vivienne Hart is this year's featured speaker?"

"Not now, Maxie. I've got a situation brewing. This joker isn't giving me the discount."

"What about my reservation?" Maxine asked.

"Was it in there? If so, maybe you can get a rollaway bed and stay with me."

Estelle's lip curled. "You snore."

"Me? You snored all the way from California. Sounded like a delivery truck stuck in low gear."

"Well," Estelle said, "that's why we should have our own rooms." She faced Finley. "Stop what you're doing and find her reservation."

"We're almost done with your check-in," the clerk said with an uneasy smile. "We should just finish."

"No." Estelle jammed her finger repeatedly onto the counter. "Look for my friend's registration right now. Maxine Coleman. We registered at the same time. If she's in the system with a discount, you're going to have a major problem."

Finley's left eye twitched.

Maxine stepped forward. "Good afternoon."

The clerk flashed a practiced smile. "Name?"

"I just told you," Estelle said. "Pay attention."

"Yes," Finley tensed. "Right." His fingers settled on the keyboard, and he stared blankly at the screen.

Maxine leaned in and slipped her driver's license across the counter.

Relief flooded the desk clerk's face. "Thank you."

"Can you believe this?" Estelle asked.

Maxine eyed her friend. "It happens. Everything will work out fine."

"Stop with the sunshine, Pollyanna." Estelle's gaze shifted to Ash. "What're you still doing here?”

“I thought your friend might need help.”

“Who are you?” Maxine asked.

“The porter.” Ash ran his hand down his burgundy vest and smiled.

“*The?* As in, the only one?”

“For today,” Ash said. “We’re shorthanded.”

Estelle harrumphed. “The outbreak.”

“Outbreak?” Maxine’s face contorted with disbelief. “What outbreak?”

“The flu. That’s why these jokers are short-staffed.”

Finley mumbled to himself, “I should never have said ‘outbreak’.” He flashed an apologetic smile at the guests standing behind Estelle. “It’s not an outbreak.”

“That’s a relief,” Maxine said.

Estelle frowned. “This’ll be the worst conference ever.”

“Maybe not.”

“Mark my words, Maxie. Worst. Conference. Ever.”

“You always say that.”

“I do not.”

“Every year,” Maxine said. “Usually during check-in.”

Estelle’s expression pickled. “I call it like I see it.”

“When it’s over, you always say it was the best conference ever.”

“Not this year.”

“I don’t care what you say, I’m going to have fun.” Maxine nodded once. “I can’t wait for tomorrow's murder mystery."

"We better win this year," Estelle said. "I'm tired of losing."

"We'll win. Have faith." Maxine looked back at the woman wearing the tight red dress. "Maybe we should ask Vivienne Hart to join our team. She's so smart."

"The others will accuse us of bringing on a ringer." Estelle looked surreptitiously over her shoulder. "Besides, the authors never take part in the murder mystery. They're always too busy to have fun."

Ash glanced at the woman in the red dress, the one he assumed was Vivienne Hart. She cocked her head as she studied Ash, a bemused look on her face. Vivienne lifted the large magnifying glass and peered through it. Her head titled and her mouth slowly opened. Ash dismissed her peculiarities since he imagined most artists were that way. How else could they come up with so many stories? He turned away from her.

"Any word about Saturday's auction?" Estelle asked.

Maxine shrugged. "No one else knows anything about the final offering. Wonder why they're keeping it a secret."

"Probably because it's going to be a big letdown."

Maxine rolled her eyes. "You're acting like Eeyore."

"Realism isn't pessimism."

"Says you." Maxine pushed her blue suitcase

toward Ash.

"What're you doing?" Estelle asked.

"He's a porter. They take our bags up to our room."

Estelle grabbed Maxine's elbow and pulled her down so they could have a private conversation. "Doesn't he look familiar?" It was supposed to be a whisper, much the way a dog barking in a junkyard is meant to be a friendly greeting.

"Now that you say it." Maxine squinted. "Who does he remind us of?"

"I don't know, and it's bugging me. I was thinking maybe we saw him on an episode of Cops or something." Estelle's lip curled. "Then I thought he might have been a model. I don't know."

"A model?" Maxine's eyes widened, and she glanced over her shoulder. She pointed at the author in the red dress. "What about Vivienne's new—?"

Estelle tugged on her friend's arm. "Until we figure it out, don't let him touch your bags."

"Okay," Maxine said, "but I'm thinking he's—"

"Uh," Finley interrupted.

"Use your words," Estelle snapped. She stood on her tiptoes again. "You don't have Maxie's reservation, either."

Finley clasped his hands together. "This never happens."

"It's happened twice." Estelle slapped the counter two times—bang, bang.

Maxine touched her friend's arm. "Maybe Phyllis forgot to send in our forms."

Estelle settled back on her heels. "I bet you're right. Is she here yet?"

"I thought so. Didn't she arrive yesterday?"

"Already got her room, I bet." Estelle glanced around. Not finding what she was looking for, she eyed Maxine. "We should get Phyllis down here to clear up this mess."

"Don't despair." Finley smiled at Maxine. "We've got one room available."

"I'll take it," Maxine said. To Estelle, she added, "See? I told you everything would work out."

"Wait." Estelle studied the desk clerk. "Are you giving her the room you promised me?"

"You passed on it."

"I did no such thing."

Finley's left eye twitched worse than before. "You didn't complete the check-in, Ms. Enderby."

Estelle huffed. "You're not suggesting we share a room?"

"No," Finley said. "Not at all."

"That's good." Estelle nodded, pleased with herself.

"Because it's Ms. Coleman's room now."

Maxine's eyes filled with delight. "You are such a wonderful young man."

"Hey." Estelle tapped her friend on the arm. "That's my room."

"He said you passed on it."

"Think about it, Maxie. Why would I give up

my room?"

"You make a lot of choices I don't understand."

Estelle pointed at Finley. "I wanted him to check your reservation, so I'd get the discount, too."

The clerk's eye twitching sped up, and a panicky titter squeaked out. "Discounts are for early registrants."

"Okay, fine," Maxine said. "What should we do about it?"

"Share it, I suppose." Estelle chopped the air with her hand. "Fifty/fifty. Right down the line."

"You said I snore."

"Probably won't hear it over my own."

"You got that right." Maxine held out her hand. "So be it. We'll split the room. That's like a fifty percent discount."

The two women shook on their agreement.

"Excellent," Finley said. "I'll put both your names on the account." His fingers ran wildly about the keyboard. "Whose credit card will this be on?"

Estelle thumbed at Maxine. "Hers."

"Mine?"

"I'll pay you back."

Maxine sighed. "You still owe me for breakfast and the cab."

"I'm good for it."

"Since you're going to the same room," Ash said as he reached for Estelle's bag, "I'll take yours as well."

She smacked his hand. "Not today, you won't."

Chapter 2

"You catch the game last night?" Ramon Martinez asked.

"I don't watch sports," Ash said.

Ramon was the hotel's concierge, a handsome man in his early forties. Unlike Ash, he didn't have to wear the hotel's uniform. He wore a green dress shirt, paisley tie, and black slacks. All things considered, Ash liked his own outfit better than what the concierge wore. He didn't have to wear a tie, and the uniform made his clothing decision easy every morning.

"You're lucky you missed it," Ramon said. "It was a horrible game. Cost me a nickel."

"Five hundred's gotta hurt."

"Tell me about it. You ever bet?"

Ash shook his head.

"Probably smart."

They were in a storage room which was unofficially the concierge office. Various pieces of luggage were stacked on steel racks. Red tags dangled from the bags, showing the owner of each. Government mandated posters hung on the walls, their subjects covering minimum wage, job safety, and employee rights. Amid the notices, someone had drawn a circle with a marker and added the words *Bang Head Here.*

"I've been wondering," Ramon said as he eyed

the silver nametag on Ash's vest. "What kind of name is Asher?"

"I don't know. What's it matter?"

"Like is it English or Scandinavian?" Ramon asked. "Because it sounds made up."

"It's not made-up."

Ramon reclined in his chair with his legs crossed and feet resting on the large metal desk. A plastic paper tray, clunky telephone, and small cardboard box covered in packing tape were the only things on its top. "Sounds like a girl's name."

"It's not," Ash said. "Lots of guys have it."

"I never met anyone with it." Ramon looked at the ceiling. "Least of all, a dude."

Ash sat on a Samsonite spinner, bent forward with his forearms on his legs. After delivering Maxine Coleman's bag to the room she shared with Estelle Enderby, he took a break to visit his cat, Travis.

The orange tom had yet to peek his head out from the nearby open cat carrier. Ash was displaced for several days because of a flood in the apartment above his. A rollaway bed in the hotel's basement was Ash's temporary home. Travis could have stayed down there during the workday, but Ash thought it better to have the cat nearby so he could occasionally check on him. Porters didn't need to go into the basement very often. The storage room seemed the best option available.

Ramon's attention remained on the ceiling. "It's probably one of those made-up millennial names like Kiernan or Jedi."

"I'm not a millennial."

The concierge's gaze fell to Ash. "You, my friend, are most definitely a millennial."

Ash had been called lots of names in life. Some true. Some not. Of all the labels he'd been called, millennial was by far the worst. He was about to express his disapproval when Travis peeked his head out of the cat carrier.

"Hey, buddy," Ash said. "You can do it."

"He's skittish, eh?" Ramon asked.

"Not normally."

"New environment, then."

Ash wriggled his fingers, hoping to encourage Travis out. He hadn't grown up around cats, so he was still getting accustomed to the animal's lack of interest in him.

Ramon asked, "You like it?"

"The cat?"

"Your name." Ramon raised an eyebrow.

"It's fine."

"Why'd your parents pick that one?"

Ash cocked his head. "Why do you care?"

"I don't," Ramon said with a shrug. "It's just that you don't seem too fond of it."

"I like it fine."

"Okay, *Ash.* Maybe you can change it. Can't be too hard to do."

Ash already knew what it felt like to change his name. He didn't want to do it again. "It is what it is."

"I suppose."

Travis left the carrier now with slow, cautious

steps. The cat ignored both men as he crept behind the first luggage rack.

"Wouldn't have taken you for a cat person," Ramon said.

"I'm not."

"Could have fooled me." The concierge lifted his chin in the direction Travis disappeared. "He do anything special?"

"Like what?"

"Fetch or something?"

"Cats don't fetch."

Ramon interlaced his hands over his stomach. "Should get a dog."

"That's the last thing I need."

"Where's its litter box?"

"In the basement."

"What if he's got to go now?"

"He already did his business this morning."

"What about toys?"

"Listen," Ash said. "It's not a perfect set-up. I'm doing the best I can." To change the topic away from his lackluster cat-parenting skills, Ash motioned toward the brown box on the desk. "What's that?"

"This?" The concierge put his hand on the cardboard container. His thumb picked at the packing tape that secured the box. "It's a manuscript."

Ash lifted slightly off the Samsonite spinner to get a better look at the package. It was unopened and a shipping label was affixed to its top. He sat again. "What's a manuscript?"

"Like a book before it becomes a book, I

guess."

"Yeah? Who wrote it?"

Ramon shrugged. "No idea, but it's supposed to be rare."

"As in?"

"Valuable." Ramon patted the box. "Worth beaucoup bucks, apparently."

Ash stretched his neck to get a better view. He only saw the hotel's address on the shipping label. He couldn't see a return address. "Whose is it?"

"Belongs to a guest." Ramon waggled his hand. "The head of the mystery conference. The President." He air-quoted the last word. "Someone shipped it here for her, and she asked me to keep watch over it."

"Why doesn't this president put it in her room safe?"

"Wouldn't fit."

"The hotel safe, then?"

"I offered." Ramon drummed his fingers on the box. "She wanted it accessible."

"Accessible?"

"Some auction they're doing to celebrate their shindig."

"That's Saturday night," Ash said, realizing whatever was in the box was likely the big secret Estelle and Maxine discussed. "You gotta keep an eye on it the whole time?"

Ramon shook his head. "Just today. Guess she'll take it after the conference starts."

Ash looked toward the ceiling. "There are no security cameras in here."

"None out there either," Ramon said. "None working at least."

"You told the conference president that?"

"Of course I did. She was already aware of it, though. Probably learned about it on a previous trip."

Cameras hung throughout the hotel, but none were hooked up. They were supposed to provide an illusion of security. Ramon had filled Ash in on the situation weeks ago. The hotel's owner was a privacy advocate and refused to record his guests. However, that decision wasn't advertised because of liability reasons. "Plus," Ramon said then, "we don't want to attract the conspiracy nuts. They only pay in cash and are terrible tippers."

In a normal circumstance, Ash might have thought the lack of security cameras an odd choice. However, he preferred not to be monitored every day. "What's a manuscript worth?" he asked.

Ramon waggled his hand. "An average one? Probably not much, I suppose. You ever been to a bookstore? Manuscripts have got to be a dime a dozen." His hand dropped to the cardboard box. "This one is special, though."

"How special?"

"Ten grand." The concierge shrugged a single shoulder. "At least, that's what the conference president said."

Ash whistled. "That much and she doesn't want it in the safe? Doesn't make sense."

"Different strokes," Ramon said. "Who knows

why people do what they do?"

"Not me." Ash rested his arm on a nearby shelf.

Ramon cocked his head and studied Ash for a couple of moments. "Got a girlfriend?"

It seemed a strange question to ask, so Ash called him on it.

The concierge shrugged. "Thought maybe we should go out sometime. You know, a double date."

"A double date? This isn't the fifties."

"Give it a rest. We can get to know each other better. Maybe catch a game. Take our girls out. Win-win." Ramon's hand continued to rub the cardboard box.

Ash didn't know Ramon had a girlfriend. The two often kept their conversations light, not revealing much about themselves. He liked that about the concierge.

"I don't have a girlfriend," Ash said. There was one woman he thought about, but Ramon wouldn't be interested in hearing Ash pine away.

The concierge bounced his thumb on the box. "You want me to fix you up with someone?"

"I'm good," Ash said.

"No man is good if he ain't got a woman." The concierge wriggled his eyebrows.

"Sounds like you got more than one."

Ramon waved a hand. "I used to have them coming out of my ears, but not now. Finally found a keeper." The concierge's eyes grew distant. "I'm letting all the others slip by the wayside."

"Got some regrets?"

"Who wouldn't?" Ramon's laugh sounded forced, like a man convincing himself vegetables tasted better than cake. "There's something wonderful in momentary relationships."

"How's that?"

"Guests." Ramon waved his hand toward the ceiling. "Ladies who stay for a day or two, then they leave. Some return the same time every season. We reconnect like long-lost lovers, then they go back home again. It's a sweet deal. You're a porter. You should know."

"I don't."

"Meeting the ladies started when I did your job."

Ash nodded slowly. "You're giving them up for one girl?"

"She's the one," Ramon said. "All others fail to compare. Ever meet anyone like that?"

Ash had but wanted to keep it to himself. So he said, "She sounds perfect." Ash knew nothing about Ramon's girlfriend but sought to move the conversation along.

"She's almost perfect," Ramon said, "except her brother. He's a real thug." The concierge shrugged a single shoulder. "Getting down to one girl means I've gotta break some hearts. Know what I'm saying? I've been an out-of-town boyfriend for so many ladies for so long it's bound to cause some hard feelings. It'll be worth it, though."

A silence fell over the small room. Ash felt

slightly guilty for sitting there when he knew the hotel was severely short-staffed. He should probably return to the lobby and help Finley.

"You know what I'm thinking?" Ramon asked. He tapped a single finger on the cardboard box as he studied it. "Maybe we should take this."

Ash furrowed his brow. "What do you mean?"

"You know. Sell it to the highest bidder ourselves. Split the cash. Seventy/thirty."

"Seventy/thirty?"

"I don't know." Ramon shrugged. "Sixty/forty?"

"You got the box. What do you need me for? Besides, how do we find the highest bidder without an auction?"

"That's a good question." Ramon examined the package. "If they're putting it up for bid, you gotta imagine there are some high rollers coming for it."

"I suppose." Ash motioned toward the box. "You sure you got no idea who wrote it?"

"None."

"Does it have a return label somewhere?"

"Nope." Ramon slid the box closer to him. "Maybe the author is a recluse, like that famous billionaire."

"Or like the Unabomber."

The concierge slowly pushed the package across the desk. "I should probably stop tapping it."

Ash turned to find Travis. The cat had disappeared behind some luggage.

"If we took it—" Ramon said.

"You're still on this?" Ash interrupted.

"If we took it," Ramon repeated, "we could open the box and find out who wrote it. Maybe learn why it's so valuable."

"Do what you want," Ash said over his shoulder, "but keep me out of it. I don't need the trouble."

"Yeah, you're right." Ramon said, the disappointment obvious in his voice. "I got enough trouble of my own." He slowly turned the box, viewing it from different angles. "Still, it would be nice to get out of the hole I dug with Mr. Leo."

Ash faced his friend again. "What hole? Who's Mr. Leo?"

The beige desk phone rang. It was an old table-top version with push buttons. Ramon slapped his hand on the lower part of the receiver, causing it to pop off the cradle and into his palm. "Concierge."

Ash shifted his position on the Samsonite to look for the cat on the bottom row of the steel shelves. Ramon snapped his fingers to get Ash's attention, then pointed at an upper shelf. Travis crept behind a duffel bag.

Ramon's feet dropped to the floor, and he stood. "Okay, sure. I'll come out." He hung up the phone. "Finley needs me."

"For?"

"Help with the guests. It's gonna be this way until the crew gets over the flu."

"Any word from Nadine?"

"She's on her way in. Sounded stuffy as all get out, but you know how managers are."

"I do."

"Not sure what she's expecting." Ramon slipped his keys into his pocket. "We've got one maintenance man, a porter, and half a cleaning staff. The day's not getting any better with a stuffed-up boss."

Ash moved a duffel bag on its shelf and grabbed Travis. "Come on, you."

"I'd let you hide out here for longer," Ramon said, "but..."

"Store policy."

Ramon laughed. "Hotel policy."

"That, too."

"I'm already pushing it by letting you keep the cat in here. He should probably be in the basement."

Ash bent and tucked the tom into the carrier. Travis trilled his displeasure at being caged again.

Ramon waited for Ash to finish, then the two men left the room. The concierge locked the unmarked door and pulled it closed behind him.

Back in the main lobby, the check-in line flowed around the corner.

Ash asked, "This mystery conference happen every year?"

"Like birds coming south for the winter." Ramon started toward the front desk. "Who even reads anymore?"

"I do." Ash felt oddly proud of the statement. It was one he wouldn't have made six months ago.

"That so?" Ramon glanced at him. "What do you read that's so interesting? Cereal boxes?"

Several children gathered at the lobby's fountain. This group threw pennies into the pool and closed their eyes. The aroma of chlorine drifted through the foyer. Overhead, "The Way You Look Tonight" played.

A woman in her early forties stood in front of the concierge desk with a cell phone pressed to her ear. Her printed dress was twisted around her waist, and her long, brown hair appeared disheveled. She waved excitedly at Ramon with her free hand.

The concierge noticed the motion and said, "Hold on," to Ash. They stopped walking as the woman hurried toward them. A name badge dangled around her neck on a lanyard. It bounced and swung with each of her steps. She ended her call as she approached the men.

Now up close, the woman's eyes widened. She hastily pulled and tugged on her dress to untwist it from her waist. "Well, hello again."

"Ma'am." Ramon smiled politely.

"Sylvia," she said as she patted her hair into place. "Please. I insist."

Ash's gaze dropped to the woman's name badge. Bold, block letters spelled out *Sylvia Grayson.* Underneath, a thin font announced she was *President—Mystery Readers of America.*

Sylvia quickly looked around and then whispered to Ramon. "How's the package?"

"Safe and sound. Locked up in the concierge

room like you asked.”

“You’re a dear.” Sylvia beamed at him.

Ash stood several inches taller than the concierge and was much larger in the shoulders, yet he might as well have been invisible. Sylvia never acknowledged his presence.

Seeing the way she ogled Ramon, Ash now knew why Sylvia asked to keep the manuscript in the concierge’s storage room.

Ramon motioned toward the front desk. “I still think the hotel safe would be a better spot for the manuscript.”

“No, no,” she said with a dismissive wave of her cell phone. “The storage room is perfect. You’re the only one with a key, right?”

“Me and the porters.” Ramon jerked his head in Ash’s direction. “We’re the only ones.”

“How many porters are there?”

“Just one today.”

Sylvia’s smile grew wider. “Well, that makes it even safer. Less people going in and out of the room.”

“I suppose.” Ramon said. “Anything else?”

“Oh, yes.” Sylvia snapped her fingers as if she suddenly remembered something. “Our signs.” She motioned toward the conference hall. “They aren’t up.”

“The stands are in place,” Ramon said. “I took care of it myself.”

“I didn’t mean to say it like that.” A fluttering smile crossed the woman’s lips. “The stands are in place.” Sylvia shifted her stance, put a hand on her hip, and cleared her throat. "Thank you for being so accommodating and all." She fanned herself with the cell phone. "Is it hot in here?"

"Not at all," Ramon said.

"Of course not." The words trailed off as Sylvia stared at the concierge. Her smile continued to tremble as a dreamy look overwhelmed her features.

"Your signs," Ramon prompted.

Sylvia blinked, and the dreaminess left her eyes. "Yes. Signs. That's right."

"What's the problem?" the concierge asked. "Perhaps we can help." He motioned toward Ash, but Sylvia still didn't bother looking at him. Her gaze remained firmly locked on the concierge.

"The directional boards haven't arrived," Sylvia said. "For the different presentations."

"They're being sent here?"

"Yes." Sylvia crossed her arms, seemed to think better of it, and let them dangle in front of her. "Or they were supposed to be." Her lips quivered in and out of a smile. "They should have arrived yesterday. I called the printer, and they said they'd rush them out."

"It'll be too late," Ramon said. "The conference starts today, right?"

"Exactly." Sylvia's head bobbed. "Exactly right. Registration starts in an hour."

"I see your dilemma."

"We can make some temporary signs," Ash offered.

For the first time, Sylvia noticed him. She pulled back as her gaze drifted up and down his frame. Her eyes eventually settled on the inky fireball covering the back of his right hand.

"Making some temporary signs is a good idea," Ramon said. To Sylvia, he asked, "Will that help?"

The woman glanced at the concierge. "Yes, that's a wonderful idea." Sylvia considered Ash once more. "I'd better do the spelling, though."

"Probably best," Ramon said. "No errors."

"What will we make the signs with?" Sylvia asked. "They're supposed to be this big." She mimed what appeared to be a square, two feet on each side.

Ramon eyed Ash. "What do you think?"

He thumbed down the hall. "There are plenty of cardboard boxes in the restaurant."

"Cardboard?" the woman asked, her nose crinkling with disdain. "Won't they smell like food?"

"The restaurant is closed for renovations," Ramon said.

Sylvia sighed. "I remember that being an issue with our scheduling this year."

"The boxes Ash is talking about are for furniture and fixtures and whatnot. They won't smell at all."

"We'll cut off the flaps," Ash said, "and get a black magic marker. People do it all the time for yard sales."

"Yard sales?" Sylvia asked. "Absolutely not. No way. We have an image to maintain." She turned to Ramon. "Don't you have a printer we can use?"

"There's one in the business center." He smiled politely. "Won't the pages be too small?"

"It's better than ugly cardboard."

"In that case," the concierge said, "you can make as many signs as you like."

"Will you help me?" Sylvia asked, her eyes widening with expectation.

"I'm needed at the front desk." Ramon motioned toward Finley. "I was on my way there. Ash will show you to the business center."

The woman's shoulders slumped.

"Good luck." Ramon waved once, then headed toward the front desk.

"Ma'am?" Ash said.

Sylvia's gaze lingered on the departing concierge.

"*Ma'am?*"

She shook her head and blinked. "Lead on."

Ash started for the south wing, where the elevator bank and conference hall were located.

Sylvia hurried to his side. They had walked for only a few seconds before she muttered, "Can this get any worse?"

"What's that?"

"Nothing," she said. "I'm feeling sorry for myself. This whole event feels cursed."

"How so?"

"I've spent the last five years working my way through the executive board. Secretary, Treasurer, you know the drill."

Ash didn't.

"This is supposed to be my moment of glory." Sylvia frowned. "After this event, my tenure as president is over. I don't want to go out with a dumpster fire of a conference."

"It can't be that bad."

"Trust me," Sylvia said. "It's worse than you know."

"What happened?"

"Everything turned sour a couple months ago when someone murdered our featured speaker."

Ash cocked his head. "No kidding?"

"Right in his home. Ever hear of Mason Freemantle?"

He stopped walking. *Mason Freemantle?*

"Of course you have," Sylvia said. "Everyone knows Mason. He was a pretty big deal for our conference, even though I'm not a fan of his work. His City series was derivative after the first book." It took Sylvia a moment to realize Ash wasn't with her anymore. She turned around. "You okay?"

"I'm fine." He started walking again.

Sylvia fell in by his side. "I'm sorry. You're probably a fan, and I just insulted him."

"I've never read his books."

"Well, that's good. I'll tell you this much. His fans are extremely loyal, but they walk the fine line of crazy. Calling themselves the Freemantles." Sylvia cast a sideways glance. "I always thought that was a ridiculous young people thing. Self-identifying with their favorite stars. Swifties. Beliebers. KatyCats. Mason's readers aren't young, though." Her eyes narrowed as she considered Ash once more. "You probably saw the movies based on his books. *The Portland Squeeze* wasn't bad. Better than the material it was based on."

"I met him," Ash said as he stopped in front of a room labeled *Business Center.* Inside the small room was a wall-length counter which held one computer and a printer. A high-back leather chair waited for an occupant.

"You met Mason?" Sylvia asked. "Where? When?"

"Chicago. A couple months ago."

"He lived there, didn't he?" she said. "You probably know all about his death."

Ash knew everything about it, in fact, but he didn't say so. Instead, he gestured toward the small room.

Sylvia stepped by him. "We advertised for most of last year that Mason was our guest speaker. With his death, we had to pivot. So, he's the inaugural Mystery Legend. Wasn't a big change, but we had to scramble to find a replacement. Luckily, Vivienne Hart was kind enough to step up. She comes every year, but she's never been our guest speaker. I've got to say, I don't know why we didn't think about it earlier. She's quite an upgrade over Mason."

"Need help with the computer?" Ash asked, hoping she would say no. He barely had any experience with them.

"I've got it." Sylvia settled into the desk chair. "One more question?"

"Ma'am?"

"I noticed Ramon wasn't wearing a wedding ring." Her cheeks flushed. "Does he have a girlfriend?"

Ash shrugged. "Sounds like he has more than a few."

"Huh." She lowered her gaze to the cell phone she held.

"I can tell him you're interested if you want."

Sylvia stiffened and turned back to the computer. "Not today, you won't."

Chapter 3

"Not today, you won't," U.S. Marshal Lester Krumland said.

"Why can't I choose?" Beauregard Smith asked.

The two were at Crawdad Park in the small town of Cameron, Louisiana, just over the state's border with Texas. The dedicated space sat on a tributary between Calcasieu Lake to the north and the Gulf of Mexico to the south. It seemed a spot the locals frequented to avoid the tourists visiting Cameron Beach for the winter.

A picnic bench stood between Beau and Krumland. A thick file sat on its top. It had grown since the last time the two men met.

The lawman jammed his finger into the open palm of his other hand. "You go where I say you go."

"Or what?" Beau asked. "You'll toss me back in the hole?"

"If I must, yes." Krumland's eyes narrowed. "It would be with some satisfaction, I might add."

Beau stared at the marshal but didn't answer. Instead, he tried to contain his anger, which was tougher than usual because of a lack of sleep.

Yesterday, a team of marshals picked up

Beau in Linda Gato, a coastal Texas town. Since then, the only shut eye he'd gotten was a quick nap in the back of an SUV. The marshals' three-vehicle caravan took backroads to this destination and often doubled-back to ensure no one was following them. His protectors woke Beau whenever he nodded off. They wanted answers concerning the recent debacle he escaped, often asking the same questions multiple times to see if his story ever changed.

It never did.

His escorts finally stopped driving when they arrived at this out-of-the-way park to meet Lester Krumland, Beau's witness inspector and the man tasked with ensuring his safety.

"I don't see the problem," Beau said. He crossed his muscular arms and set his jaw. "I only want some say in where I end up. You don't have to be unreasonable about it."

"Keep pushing, and you'll find out just how unreasonable I can be."

Krumland was a big man, standing eye to eye with Beau. The marshal wore a tan suit too large for his large frame. It hung loosely from his shoulders and billowed around his rotund waist. A golden clip pinned a striped necktie to Krumland's white shirt. A miniature American flag was affixed to the suit's lapel. The lawman hadn't lost weight since the last time Beau saw him. Instead, the ill-fitting clothes appeared to be off the rack, much like the suit the marshal wore during their previous encounter.

The marshal's appearance was in stark

contrast to Beau's black T-shirt, blue jeans, and combat boots. If anyone noticed them, they might think it was a moderately successful defense attorney talking to a client. They wouldn't be far off in that assessment.

Krumland continued. "My job is to keep you alive and safe, so we're stuck together. I don't like it any more than you."

A group of small children played nearby on the tributary's muddy shore. Twenty yards away and equal distance from where Beau and Krumland met, a cluster of parents sipped coffee from steel travel mugs and ignored their progeny. Even though Beau couldn't make out the parents' conversation, he could hear their haughty laughs. He immediately knew he wouldn't like any of them and for more reasons than their choices to procreate.

Krumland dropped heavily onto the picnic bench, straddling his seat. "Let me ask you something." He rested an arm along the tabletop. "Are you purposefully tanking your assignments?"

"You talking about Lindo Gato?"

"I'm talking about all of them, but let's start with Lindo Gato."

Beau sat across from Krumland. "The mob was there."

The marshal smirked. "Surprise, surprise. You found them. Funny how that works whenever you're around."

"I was minding my own business."

"Then why are we here?" Krumland waggled

his hand. "Go on, smart guy. Tell me."

"They were going to kill me."

Krumland stared silently at Beau.

The children squealed with delight near the water as their parents toasted themselves in the grassy area. The sound of clanging travel mugs reverberated through the park.

"Me getting killed would be bad," Beau said, "in case you're not picking that up."

"Yes, of course. That would be bad." The marshal grunted before looking away. "Definitely bad." It didn't sound convincing.

"I'm not doing this on purpose," Beau said.

"That so?" Krumland watched his charge from the corner of his eye. "Sure seems like you want to get caught."

"That already happened."

The FBI arrested Beau months ago. He'd been the bookkeeper for the Satan's Dawgs, a motorcycle club based out of Phoenix, Arizona. The crew used coded nicknames for various responsibilities. Beau's job was to "keep book" on those who crossed the Dawgs. The leadership frequently called the accounts due, always with interest paid in the form of physical pain. Sometimes they ordered Beau to close an account. He did that better than anyone in the club's history.

"You're right," Krumland said. "You *were* caught. Maybe you should think about that and find the common denominator."

An FBI agent offered Beau a way out of his trouble—turn rat on the club. The fed also dangled the threat of incarcerating Beau's grandmother, the only person he truly loved. Beau had paid off her mortgage and renovated her house with money earned through the club's illegal activities. The government planned to charge her as an accessory to the Dawg's escapades if Beau didn't help.

He never had a choice.

On the shore, the children jammed their hands into the mud and threw it at each other. Laughs and playful shrieks didn't attract the attention of any parent. Instead, the adults blissfully drank their coffee and laughed loudly, as if there were no problems in the world.

Turning on his club wasn't as hard as Beau might have thought. The Dawgs had lost their way, changing from a brotherhood to a profit-driven entity, just like a greedy corporation. Beau knew it was time to go when the leadership started lending out his skills to other clubs for money. The FBI's heavy-handed offer was the lifeline he hadn't known he needed.

"I don't want to sound like a wimp," Beau said, "but you guys promised to protect me."

Krumland faced him. "You have to do your part, Beau."

He turned his palms upward. "How am I not?"

"Seven blown covers."

"We've been over this."

"It was six the last time we talked. All lost in a matter of months, I might add."

"It's been a bad run."

"A bad run?" Krumland scoffed. "Losing six

hands of blackjack in a row is a bad run. You're on a hot streak of terrible. If life was a casino, we'd suspect you of counting cards with the intent to lose."

Beau furrowed his brow. "Huh?"

"You get my meaning." The lawman dismissively waved his hand.

Near the water, the children stopped throwing mud at each other. They huddled together, some furtively glancing at their unaware parents.

Beau dragged his attention from the kids and focused on the marshal. "I've been wondering something."

Krumland inhaled slowly, held his breath for a moment, then exhaled. "I don't want to hear it."

"How could you not know the Outfit was in Lindo Gato?"

The marshal awkwardly spun on his seat, bringing both legs underneath the picnic table. Hatred burned in his eyes. "You making this about me?"

"Well—"

"Because this is about you." Krumland's hand fell heavily on the file. "All you."

"I think you have some responsibility in this matter."

"You've got some nerve. I'll give you that." The marshal's back straightened and his expression tightened. "The last time we met—" Krumland's voice filled with anger and righteous indignation. It was the tone cops used when they falsely accuse someone of a crime. "—you said the previous screw-ups weren't the responsibility of your other witness inspectors. Somehow, this one is mine?"

Beau rested his elbows on the table and leaned forward. "You gotta admit, you should've known the Outfit was operating there."

"We wouldn't even have to worry about the mob or any of its offshoots if you hadn't stirred up a hornet's nest in Maine." Krumland flipped open the folder. "Should I remind you of those events?"

"No. I got it."

Krumland flipped a couple more pages. "What about California? It wasn't me who attracted the media's attention. It was you." He cocked his head. "Am I wrong?"

"Okay," Beau said. "We're getting sideways."

"You bet we're getting sideways." Krumland angrily turned more pages in the file. "Here! Right here. You found trouble in Eagle's Feet, Wyoming. That's the middle of nowhere, Beau. How does that happen?"

"Maybe I was hasty with my accusation."

"You think?" Krumland slapped the file closed, then put his head in his hands with his elbows resting on the picnic table. "Your actions are dragging me down."

Beau believed the marshal was on the agency's hot seat, this witness inspector assignment being punishment for some misdeed. He wanted to know what Krumland had done wrong.

Twenty yards away, the children silently ran up from the muddy shore like a group of invading Vikings. They clutched clumps of mud in their small hands and raised them above their heads. The unsuspecting parents continued to enjoy their coffee, chuckling self-righteously, like a bunch of conspiring businessmen. Probably congratulating themselves for their child-rearing skills, Beau thought.

Krumland said something, but Beau ignored it. His concentration remained on the horde of children. They screamed together like little warriors unleashing a collective fury. The kids hurled sludge at their parents. The adults screamed and ran, holding their steel travel mugs high in the air.

After the shock of the attack wore off, the parents tittered amongst themselves. The pack of children retreated to the muddy beach.

"You hear what I'm telling you?" Krumland asked.

Beau eyed him now. "Say it again."

"You're only getting one more chance." The marshal held up a finger. "Understand? Screw up this assignment, and I'll see to it you're out of the program."

"It's nice to know the marshals are in my corner."

"Seven covers, Beau. It's not normal. No one I've known has ever had more than two, and that was considered a major failure for the agency."

Beau started to protest but thought better of it. "Fine," was all he said.

"Keep your head down." Lester Krumland jammed his finger against the top of the picnic table. "Stay out of trouble. Really. Why does it have to be harder than that?"

Chapter 4

Nadine Delacroix entered the main lobby and immediately blew her nose in a tissue. She wore a light green pantsuit with a black shirt. A beige, slouchy purse hung from her right shoulder. Her eyes cut toward the concierge's desk. Much of her face remained obscured behind the tissue. Almost immediately, the hotel manager's gaze swept over the scene of registering guests and fountain-obsessed children before landing on Ash.

He had just returned from showing Sylvia Grayson to the business office and now lingered near the check-in counter. Nadine nodded once as both her hands held the tissue in front of her nose. Ash lifted his hand in acknowledgment.

Nearby, Finley Hester chatted with Enoch and Loretta Mayfield, an Arkansas couple checking into the hotel. Ash heard their names when they started the registration process.

Enoch might have been in his early eighties. He wore a long-sleeved plaid shirt with brown slacks belted high above his waist. Loretta seemed many years her husband's junior, perhaps in her mid-sixties. She wore ruby slacks and a beige sweater.

"I'm gonna have another birthday before we get this done," the husband grumbled.

Loretta smirked. "Your birthday is tomorrow."

"I mean another one after that."

Finley stopped typing long enough to glance at the ID card sitting next to his keyboard. "Happy birthday," he said. His practiced smile clanged against his halfhearted tone.

"Settle down," Enoch said. His gaze shifted to Ash. "What're you looking at?"

"I'm the porter."

"Didn't answer my question."

Ash pointed at the couple's two bags. They were different sizes but the same color and make, as if they had come in a set. "I'm here to help you to your room."

"We don't need any help," Enoch said. "We're more than capable."

Loretta patted her husband's arm. "It's his job."

"Let him do it somewhere else."

Across the lobby, Nadine wiped her nose a final time with the tissue and shoved it into her purse. She glanced once more at the unstaffed concierge desk, then walked over to the storage room where she tugged on the locked handle. She knocked on the door.

A moment later, it opened, and Ramon stuck his head out. He seemed surprised by Nadine's presence but quickly relaxed. He glanced both ways, then pulled the door fully open so Nadine could enter. The concierge's gaze swept the lobby once more before he stepped back and closed the door.

"You look familiar," Loretta said to Ash,

pulling his attention to her. She squinted. "Where do I know you from?"

It was the second time today someone had accused him of looking familiar. Unfortunately, Ash had been splashed over many social media platforms during the past couple of months. He doubted this couple saw his fight on a California boardwalk or the livestream from the Wyoming convenience store. Maybe they saw him on a news report. For a guy trying to maintain a low profile, he was doing a poor job of it.

"I have that kind of face," Ash said.

"That's not it." Loretta eyed her husband. "He look familiar to you?"

"Put on your glasses."

She smacked Enoch's arm. "I see him fine." She squinted once more while studying Ash. "I swear I know you."

Enoch rolled his eyes. "They all look the same."

Ash cocked his head. *They all?*

The older man must have sensed Ash's confusion. He waved off the confusion. "Don't get your knickers in a bunch. I meant you waiter-ly types."

"Porter," Ash corrected.

"Don't be thick," Enoch said. "You got my drift."

Loretta waggled a finger. "I'm not wrong. I've seen him somewhere before. Like in a magazine, maybe."

Finley leaned toward the couple. "All right. I just need a credit card for incidentals."

Enoch looked at his wife. "Didn't we put that in the computer when we registered?"

Loretta pulled her attention from Ash. "What's that?"

"When we registered," Enoch said, "didn't we put in our credit card?"

"We did. Of course."

The desk clerk smiled. "That was to book the room."

"What're we doing now?" Enoch asked.

"Registering," Finley said with a twitching smile.

Enoch crinkled his nose. "What's the difference?"

"Just give him the card," Loretta said, "and stop arguing, you cheapskate." She looked back at the other guests in line. "Busy today."

"Yes, ma'am," Finley said. "It's the mystery readers' conference."

The door to the concierge's small room opened and Nadine exited. Once more, Ramon stuck his head out and hurriedly surveyed the lobby. He stepped back and shut the door.

Nadine crossed the lobby, her purse bouncing against her hip. The bag appeared heavier now. The hotel manager disappeared into the north hallway.

"Mystery conference?" Loretta asked. "That sounds like fun."

"Like a root canal." Enoch slapped his credit card onto the counter.

"Maybe we should go? I like to read."

"You read romance books."

"Vivienne Hart doesn't write romance books, dear. She writes romantic mysteries." Loretta's gaze snapped to Ash. "Hey, that's where I know—"

"Vivienne Hart is here," Finley interrupted.

Loretta's head whipped around, and she bent toward the desk clerk. "Vivienne's here?" she asked. "No fooling?"

"I think she's a guest speaker," Finley said. "Or something."

Mrs. Mayfield faced her husband. "Did you hear that?"

"I'm standing right here," Enoch said, his expression pickling. "If you wanna go, then go. Help yourself."

Loretta eyed Ash. "I can't wait to ask her about—"

"Mother," Enoch interjected, "how many times have I told you? Stop selling when you get a yes."

Mrs. Mayfield studied Ash for a second longer before turning her attention back to her husband. "You sure you don't mind?"

"As long as I don't have to go. I'm not missing the Captain Marlowe tour for nothing. That's the whole reason we came here."

"That's wonderful." Loretta beamed. "Vivienne Hart," she said wistfully. "The Queen of Dream."

Enoch shrugged. "It's no skin off my nose if you don't wanna go with me. I'll do the tour alone."

Loretta frowned. "You old goat. You said it

was okay for me to skip it."

"Bah." He sounded like a disinterested sheep. "Do what you like."

A man entered the main lobby and headed for the concierge desk. He wore a black leather jacket over the top of a white hooded sweatshirt, faded jeans, and black boots. His black hair was slicked back and his five o'clock shadow appeared manicured.

Ash pointed at the Mayfields' bags. "You sure you don't need any help?"

"We're old," Enoch said. "Not feeble."

"Be nice." Loretta smiled apologetically at Ash. "We appreciate the offer, and I think I know where I saw you." Her grin widened. "You're on—"

Enoch tugged on his wife's arm. "Leave him alone, Mother. He's got work to do."

Ash nodded politely at the couple, then started for the concierge desk.

The man in the leather jacket glanced around, his face looked tight with anger.

"Can I help you?" Ash asked.

"Where's Ramon?"

"He's not here."

"Cute." The new arrival sucked air through his teeth. He leaned in and read Ash's name tag. "That's your name?" He chuckled. "Your father lose a bet?"

Ash studied the man. He had an immediate impression the guy wasn't staying at the hotel.

"What're you supposed to be?" the new arrival asked.

"The porter. You?"

"They dress you like a valet." The man glanced around. "Where'd Ramon go?"

"I don't know," Ash lied. He refused to look at the storage room. "Maybe he got called away."

"Think again. Ramon knew I was going to be here at this time." The man pointed at the floor. "He's around here somewhere." His eyes narrowed. "Let me rephrase that. He *better* be around here."

Ash crossed his arms. "Or else?"

"That's right." The man bared his teeth and curled his hand into a fist. "Or else."

"If I see Ramon, who should I say is looking for him?"

"You getting smart?"

Ash cocked his head. "Why is it you types always ask that question?"

"What question?"

"I need your name in case I see Ramon."

"Uh-huh." The man pulled his shoulders back and enlarged his chest like a cobra unfurling its hood. "Call me Knuckles. That's all you need to know."

Ash didn't bother hiding his smile.

"That funny?" Knuckles asked. His shoulders returned to their normal position, and his chest lost its extra girth.

"Does he know what this is regarding?"

"Now you sound like an operator."

Ash stared at him.

"Yeah," Knuckles said. "He knows what this is regarding." He waggled his fist. "You should probably figure it out, too."

Ash lifted an eyebrow. "Are you here for Mr. Leo?" He recalled the name Ramon mentioned earlier while they were sitting in the storage room.

"Look at you, a regular smart guy."

"How much is Ramon into Mr. Leo for?"

"None of your business. That's how much."

"When you put it that way," Ash said. "Does Ramon have your number?"

"Nobody gets my number." Knuckles glared at Ash. "I'm the one who gets the numbers. Not the other way around. Understand?"

"Better than you know."

Knuckles dropped his scowl. "I'll tell you what." He flicked the end of his nose with a thumb. "I think I'm gonna hang around for a bit. See if maybe I run into him."

"Have it your way."

"I always do." He leaned an elbow on the concierge desk. "Now, toddle off."

Ash didn't move. He didn't like being dismissed by goons like Knuckles. In his old life, Ash would likely have challenged this man. Heck, it might not have even come to that. Ash might have sucker-punched the guy. Unfortunately, that was behavior he couldn't engage in any longer.

His first marshal gave him some simple directions to help ensure his success in the program.

Do not contact people from your old life.
Do not visit places from your old life.

Do not develop habits from your old life.

Ash tried to live by the rules, but trouble kept finding him. He couldn't let it happen today.

"Wanna start something?" Knuckles asked.

"Not me," Ash said.

"That's what I thought."

Ash forced a smile. "Have a nice day."

He turned and headed for the front desk.

***

Thelma Bennett was in her mid-seventies. She wore black slacks, sparkling gold shoes, and a black sweatshirt printed with a smiling worm wearing reading glasses and the tagline *Beautiful Bookworms*. Thelma had two suitcases, one of which was exceptionally heavy.

"I apologize for that one," Thelma said when they entered the elevator. She motioned at the heavy bag. "It's full of books."

Ash pressed the appropriate floor number, and the elevator doors closed. "Mysteries?"

"Of course." Thelma smiled. "I read nothing else. My friends and I bring books to trade when we're away from the conference." Her smile turned conspiratorial. "The powers that be discourage the practice. They want us buying the new books the authors bring. Can't say as I blame them."

The elevator moved slowly upward.

Thelma continued. "My daughter is on her way from Jacksonville right now. At the end of the conference, I give her the books I didn't trade. It's sort of tradition now."

Ash smiled respectfully.

"Do you read?" Thelma asked.

"Some." He leaned his back against the elevator rail. "John D. MacDonald. Richard Stark."

"Those old fogeys?" Thelma chuckled. "I know, I know. Kettle and pot, am I right?" She waved as her titter petered out. "There are so many new writers you should try. Klein, Mulhern, and Clark are some of my favorites, but you might want to try—"

The elevator doors opened on the sixth floor, the hotel's uppermost. The two stepped out.

A few doors down the hall, Emily Larson stood next to a cleaning cart. She was in her early thirties, with short dark hair and kind eyes. Even though they'd seen each other around the hotel, Emily never spoke to him except to say hello and thank you. She might have been the shyest woman Ash had ever met. Right now, Emily was the only member of the cleaning staff working because of the flu wave.

Ash couldn't see much beyond Emily since the corridor bent. The north corridor did the same. From outside, the hotel's curvature was hard to see. If Ash could see it from the air, he'd imagine the hotel's design resembled a bird with outstretched wings. Unfortunately, he arrived in Marlowe Bay by SUV, so he never saw the city from above.

Emily nodded in Ash's direction, then grabbed a fresh set of linens and disappeared into an open room.

Thelma continued to rattle off authors Ash had never read. He stopped listening as they proceeded toward her room. When the two reached her door, Thelma said, "I could go on all day."

She unlocked the room, and Ash wheeled in her luggage. There were two beds and a view of the ocean.

"Thank you for the recommendations," Ash said politely. "Would you like me to lift either of these bags onto a bed?"

"That's okay. My daughter can help when she gets here."

"All right, then. Let us know if you need anything."

Thelma lifted a finger, silently asking him to wait. "Are you working all weekend?"

"I am."

Her smile broadened. "Oh boy, you're a lucky duck. You'll get to meet so many authors. You should wander around when you have a break and talk with some of them. Maybe find someone new to read."

"How many times have you been to this conference?" Ash asked.

"Since the first. Twenty-one times." Thelma beamed. "I'm an Enigma. That's what they call someone who's been to every event." She held her hand next to her mouth like she was sharing a secret. "It's not the right use of the term, I know, but the planning committee needed something that sounded mysterious."

Ash had heard the word before but didn't know the definition. He decided to believe Thelma's take on it.

Thelma continued. "The only others to have earned the title are a couple of Mystery Mavens." Her eyes narrowed. "Our nemesis." She abruptly cocked her head. "Or is it nemeses?"

Ash didn't know the difference, so he asked, "Have all the conferences been here?"

"Not at this hotel, no. Only the last five or so, but the conference has always been in Marlowe Bay. The head of our conference is friends with the hotel manager here. They gave us a deal several years back and we've been loyal ever since."

"Why hold a conference here?" Ash asked. "Why not Atlanta or Jacksonville? Those cities are close and there's a lot more to do."

"Isn't it obvious?"

He stared at her.

"Philip Marlowe." When that didn't register with Ash, Thelma added, "Raymond Chandler."

"I don't know who they are."

"For a fan of the fogeys, you're missing out. Philip Marlowe is Chandler's private detective. He was in books like *The Big Sleep*, *The Little Sister*, and *The Long Goodbye*." She ticked off each reference by holding up a corresponding finger. "All made into movies, by the way."

He hadn't seen those films either. "So, they named this city after a made-up detective?" Ash asked.

"Heaven's no." Thelma laughed. "It was

named after Captain John Marlowe, a skipper for the British East India Company who avoided the Boston Tea Party only to run his ship aground here, cracking its stern. Pretty crazy, huh? Anyway, the sailors scuttled the ship before swimming to shore. When they made it to the sandy banks, the first thing Marlowe's men did was hang him."

Ash raised an eyebrow. "Strange to name a town after an incident like that."

"They originally called it Swing Town, so there's that."

"Marlowe Bay is much better."

"Didn't hurt the tourism industry." Thelma patted the heavy bag. "I'll tell you what. I think I have a Chandler book in here. When I open it up, I'll put it aside for you, seeing as how you enjoy reading the classics." She winked.

Ash didn't know enough about the mystery genre to consider MacDonald or Stark truly classic. Their stories took place in the sixties and seventies, so maybe that's what made them masterpieces.

"Have a pleasant stay," Ash said, then headed toward the hallway.

***

He returned to the main lobby. Ash glanced toward the concierge desk, but Ramon still wasn't there. The lobby's fountain was free of chattering children, a fact Ash took as a good sign. His route to the front desk tightened as he walked by the feature. Not believing in the power of wishing, he hadn't thrown a coin into the water yet. He marveled at the amount of change at the bottom of the small pool.

The registration line had grown with waiting guests, who alternated their glances between the front desk and their watches.

From behind his computer, Finley eyed the approaching Ash. "You sure you're not holding out on some computer skills?"

Ash could hunt and peck if needed. Computer skills weren't required for membership in the Satan's Dawgs. The club's younger prospects and the hang-around girls always took care of those demands.

The couple now standing at the front desk eyed Ash. He smiled, but the gesture was unreturned. The man checked his watch, whispered something to his wife, then returned his withering gaze to Finley.

"Ramon hasn't come out of the storage room?" Ash asked.

Finley looked toward the concierge desk. "Didn't know he was in there. Maybe he got called away."

"What about Nadine?"

"What about her?"

"She's here," Ash said.

Finley's face pinched. "She came in?"

"You didn't know?"

"How would I?"

"Ramon told me she was on her way in," Ash said. "I saw her before I took the last customer up."

Finley furrowed his brow. "That's strange. No one told me." Finley turned his attention to the waiting couple. "Just a minute more, folks. Sorry for the delay." His fingers settled on the keyboard, but he looked up at Ash. "Maybe Nadine will help with the check-ins."

Ash scanned the lobby, looking for the tough guy named Knuckles. He didn't see him either.

"Something else?" Finley absently asked Ash.

"A guy in a leather jacket. Hooded sweatshirt underneath."

"Haven't seen him either. You're keeping tabs on a lot of folks."

"A porter's work," Ash said.

Finley eyed the couple. "Just need a credit card."

The man reached into his back pocket and pulled out his wallet.

"I'm going to head over to the storage room," Ash said, "and check on my cat."

"These guests will need help to their room."

The husband and wife pushed their bags toward Ash.

"You might get to work a double shift," Finley said. He handed the credit card back to the waiting man. "Since you're spending the night and all."

Ash shrugged. He had nothing else to do. He didn't have friends or outside hobbies to keep him busy. When he was with the Dawgs, he'd while away the time with one of the hang-around girls. He refused to do that now because of a woman he met in Pleasant Valley, Maine. She continued to linger in his memory. It was a pleasant sensation Ash didn't want to sully.

"This will be a long weekend," Finley muttered, "if we don't get some more help soon."

"Skeeter?" a woman whispered.

Ash spun, recalling the name he recently lived under while in Chicago. His eyes widened when recognition set in.

Carrie Fenton smiled, and the corner of her eyes crinkled. "It is you."

A purse hung from her left shoulder while her right clung to a large suitcase. Carrie wore a light jean jacket over a red shirt. Her jeans had holes in the knees and her red Converse appeared new.

"Who's Skeeter?" Finley asked over the top of his computer.

"Never mind," Ash said. He gently grabbed the woman's arm to escort her away from the line.

"Wait a second." Carrie grabbed her suitcase. It rolled loudly across the tile.

"Where're you going?" Finley whined. "These folks need help."

"I'll be right back," Ash said.

The line of waiting guests watched him lead Carrie away.

"Are you using the Brody name again?" she whispered. "I really liked that one."

He first met Carrie during his ill-fated time in Maine. Even though she wrote a handful of true-crime novels set within the state, Carrie felt she never had a true understanding of her subject.

She befriended a woman with a criminal history, and the two robbed a local mobster. That's when things took a bad turn for Ash, and he blew his cover trying to help the women.

Ash tugged Carrie along, moving to the edge of the main lobby. His eyes swept back and forth, looking for anyone who might have heard her use two of his previous aliases. He also looked for Ramon, Nadine, and Knuckles. He didn't see any of them.

"I can't believe it's really you," Carrie said as she tried to keep up with Ash.

Finding a quiet spot, he spun around. "What're you doing here?" he asked. Concern laced every word.

Carrie shook her head, confused. "I'm here for the conference. It's the only reason I would ever come to Marlowe Bay."

Ash looked over her shoulder to the lobby. "The mystery reader conference," he said with a withering sigh.

"That's right. I'm the non-fiction guest speaker." Carrie's gaze dropped to the nametag pinned to his chest. "Asher? Who's picking these names? Tell me it's not you."

He glanced about again to make sure no one was approaching.

"Because somebody must hate you," Carrie said.

Ash leaned close and whispered. "You can't use my other names here."

Carrie frowned. "I'm not stupid. I get how the program works." Her face tightened further.

"Hey! Did you hear about Mason Freemantle? The MRA is giving him a posthumous award."

Ash nodded. "The Legend."

"I know, right? Isn't that the most horrendous thing you've ever heard?"

It wasn't, but admitting so wouldn't help change her opinion of the famous author.

Freemantle stole a book idea from Carrie Fenton, then turned it into a bestseller. He wound up murdered at an upscale senior community where Ash previously worked. Carrie was there visiting her grandmother. The cops suspected Carrie's involvement because of an earlier run-in with the bestselling novelist. Ash helped her get free of the police but burned another identity in the process.

Carrie tsked. "After Mason's murder, the planning committee voted to create an award for him." She smirked. "I'm just glad they didn't name it after him." She lowered her voice into a mocking tone. "Congratulations, you won. Here's your Freemantle. Put it on your mantle."

Ash glanced around, looking for anyone eavesdropping on their conversation.

"What're you doing here?" Carrie asked. "Are you a waiter or something?"

He tugged on the bottom of his burgundy vest. "Porter."

"Look at you," Carrie said with an appreciative smile. "Bookstore owner, maintenance guru, hotel porter. You're a regular Renaissance man."

Ash sighed. "Listen—"

"Oh, wait!" Carrie grabbed his upper arms. "I just realized you don't know the best part. Guess who came with me?"

Behind her, a woman entered the hotel and stopped just inside the doors. Her golden hair was tucked under a black bucket hat. She wore a heavy sweater over a printed dress. Round glasses sat perched on the end of her nose.

Ash noticed the woman immediately and inhaled sharply.

Daphne Winterbourne smiled, her eyes taking in the fountain and the other ornate work in the main lobby. With a single finger, she pushed the glasses back up her nose. Daphne was the woman Ash had fallen for while living in Maine, the woman who he couldn't stop thinking about these last few months, the woman his past put into incredible danger.

"You remember Daphne, right?" Carrie asked. "From Pleasant Valley?"

Ash crouched low, hiding.

"What's wrong?" The author looked over her shoulder. "There she is." The writer waved, then turned back and looked down at Ash. "What's wrong?"

"Daphne can't know I'm here," he whispered hurriedly.

"Why not? She won't tell anyone."

Ash peeked around Carrie. Daphne headed their way. "It's too dangerous," he said. "Say nothing."

He spun and ran toward the conference hall, hunched like a soldier escaping incoming fire.

Chapter 5

A whirring moan droned loudly throughout the basement. The hotel's air system struggled as it heated the building.

Ash sat on the edge of a rollaway bed in the basement, his elbows on his knees. This was supposed to be his home for a few days while his apartment was repaired because of its flood damage. Next to him was a Karate Kitty kicker toy for the cat and the latest book he was reading—Richard Stark's *Slayground*.

A litter box sat several feet away. Maybe Ash should have let Travis roam freely through the basement. However, the cat tended to get into things and cause a mess. Ash thought he needed to supervise the tom while it wandered down here because of sharp and dangerous tools. Perhaps he worried too much. Travis surely wasn't having a good time being locked inside a cat carrier in the concierge room.

Not that any of it mattered now.

Bang.

The loud noise pulled Ash from his thoughts, and he looked up.

Hubert Dunn stood in front of a workbench. He swung a hammer, pounding its head against a piece of metal. *Bang, bang.* Hubie tossed the tool to the side, then admired the bent piece of steel.

Next to the workbench, four radio charging stations hung on the wall. Each station had six charging docks. Employees clocked in at the start of their shift and grabbed a radio. At the end of the day, they clocked out and slipped the handheld device back into an open dock. Almost all the hotel radios were currently charging.

Also mounted on the wall was an antiquated time clock. It had a gray metallic case and made a chunking sound when stamping timecards. The hotel's ownership believed the system kept their employees honest. Ash knew many of the employees had others clock in and out for them.

No system was foolproof if someone wanted to be dishonest.

The radio clipped to Ash's belt beeped before Finley Hester's voice came through. It squawked whenever the device switched to a new channel.

"*Ramon*," the desk clerk said, "*please respond.*" It was the third call for Ramon in the last couple of minutes.

Hubie glanced over his shoulder. "Unlike Ramon not to answer. Maybe he's in the head."

A balding man in his early sixties, Hubie was the hotel's lead maintenance engineer. Everything about him was gray. His wrinkled skin was colored like an afternoon shadow, the longish hair on the sides of his head resembled a dusty broom, and his uniform looked like wet gravel.

Ash liked Hubie. In fact, he liked all the maintenance men working for the hotel. Ash was once employed in the same profession. It only lasted a few days while he lived in Chicago. Still, he felt an affinity for the vocation.

"Maybe," Ash agreed to the suggestion Ramon was in the restroom. He wasn't in a talking mood and, despite liking Hubie, didn't want to encourage conversation with the man.

The maintenance man turned his attention back to the bent piece of metal. "Must be something big for the front desk to call so many times."

Ash shrugged a single shoulder, a gesture Hubie couldn't see. "Finley's acting manager."

"Doesn't sound like he's handling it well."

"Won't be much longer," Ash said. "Nadine's back."

"Thought she had the crud." Hubie wiped one hand over the workbench, knocking some screws into the open palm of the other. "Good for her, though. Pushing through. Too many call out sick for the sniffles."

Ash had never called out sick while with the Satan's Dawgs. Not that it would matter. The club didn't give sick time and holidays were only observed when convenient. Every day was a workday, a chance to make money or get even.

"Plumbers' tape," Hubie grumbled to himself. "Are we really out? Why doesn't anyone ever leave a note?"

"*Ash,*" Finley said over the radio, his voice raising in alarm. "*What about you? Please report in.*"

Ash put his head in his hands now. His eyes

caught the end of a small travel bag stowed underneath the low bed. It contained Ash's change of clothes, his cell phone, and a knitting kit. The latter was for stress relief, a skill taught to him by his grandmother. He never carried the phone while working.

He bought the flip-phone at a convenience store a block from his apartment and paid for a handful of minutes. The cheap device, commonly known as a burner, could be broken and discarded. No record of ownership or service contract would ever tie Ash to it.

Ash didn't store numbers in the phone, a practice learned while with the club and honed since his placement in the Witness Protection Program. He only needed two contacts anyway, and he logged both numbers to memory—the U.S. Marshal's emergency hotline and the FBI agent who originally arrested him.

Hubie turned around. He wiped his hands on a greasy rag. "Going to get that?"

Ash looked through his fingers at the maintenance man.

"Front desk is calling for you now," Hubie said.

"I'll get it in a minute."

"The keyboard punchers don't like waiting."

Ash stared at the man without commenting.

"We maintenance monkeys would never get away with not answering. Management insists on a salute and a smile." Hubie stiffened and brought his hand up to his eyebrow, a perfect military acknowledgment. "Private Hubert

Dunn reporting as ordered."

"It's not that bad," Ash muttered.

Hubie dropped his hand. "How would you know? Life is different for lobby folks."

Two seconds passed without Ash biting on the older man's comments.

"Doesn't make no never mind to me. Go ahead and ignore the call." Hubie balled the greasy rag and stuffed it into his back pocket. "Not gonna affect me none."

"I need a moment to think," Ash said finally.

"Won't get many of those today, what with us being down most of the crew." Hubie cocked his head. "What's wrong with you? We've been busy before. Maybe not this crazy, but it'll work out."

Ash studied his open hands. "Today's different."

"You're not gonna go home sick, are you?" Hubie's eyes filled with judgement. "Got a tickle in your throat, princess?"

"It's not like that."

"All right, all right. I get it." Hubie flicked his hand in Ash's direction. "Don't tell an old man nothin'." He walked over to the workbench and grabbed his tool belt. He slipped it around his waist. "I gotta make a repair on three anyway. I'll leave you to your thoughts."

The older man sauntered away. A hammer handle bounced against the side of his leg with each step.

With the back of his boot, Ash pushed the little bag further under the bed.

He hated hiding. It certainly wasn't the first

time he stayed out of sight. When he was with the Satan's Dawg's, hiding from the cops was a common occurrence. The club even hid from rival gangs when they weren't ready for a clash.

Ash thought his days of hiding were over after the FBI hauled him in. Since joining the Witness Protection Program, he hid more now than he ever did wearing a Satan's Dawgs' cut, the leather vest with the demonic dog on its back.

"Anyone seen Ash or Ramon?" Finley asked. *"Someone report in."*

"I saw Ash on six," Emily Larson responded.

"When was this?"

"Fifteen minutes ago," the housekeeper said. *"Maybe."*

Ash turned down the radio, so it was barely audible.

"Was he with Ramon?" Finley asked.

"No, sir."

Once again, Ash's world had turned upside down. At least this time, he'd been in place more than a month. Could he stay here after seeing Carrie Fenton and Daphne Winterbourne? He knew the unpleasant answer but was hesitant to call the marshal's hotline and report the problem.

Marshal Lester Krumland threatened to end Ash's time in the program if he blew another assignment. If the lawman did that, Ash might end up behind bars again. As part of his agreement to turn against the club, Ash's sentence was suspended. The program acted as a surrogate probation. If Ash was sent back to prison, the Satan's Dawgs and the mob could easily reach him. They would have unfettered access to him if he was incarcerated anywhere, even if they didn't have men of their own behind that particular set of bars.

In the criminal world, favors were done for various reasons. One corrupt hand washed the other. Perhaps those favors were banked for later use. Most often, they were exchanged concurrently. A confirmed rat would die in prison before he could do any more damage while, at the same time, a suspected rat was permanently removed from the streets. The crimes remained unsolved because the killer and victim were only linked by a couple of favors, forever kept secret.

Ash's situation wouldn't be any better if they just kicked him out of the program. He'd have no one watching his back. Surely the Dawgs or the mob would find him eventually.

Yet a quick exit from the Witness Protection Program wasn't the only reason for Ash's hesitancy to call the emergency hotline. He wanted to see Daphne once more. He shouldn't talk with her because that might invite danger back into her life. Daphne was kidnapped once because of their connection, an action that resulted in the death of an east coast gangster and the mob joining the Satan's Dawgs' hunt for Ash.

The best Ash could do for everyone was grab his cell phone and leave. Slink out the back of the hotel, find a dark alley somewhere, and wait for the marshals to arrive. Still, he had to see Daphne again, even if it was from a distance.

His eyes dropped to the kicker toy on his bunk. He also couldn't leave Travis.

"Hello? Anyone?" Finley asked, his voice reaching a hysterical level. *"Someone report in."*

"Might try checking the basement," Hubie said.

"Hubie?" Finley asked. *"Are Ramon and Ash there?"*

"Don't know," the maintenance man said. *"Just making a suggestion."*

"Can you check?"

"I'm headed to three. Gonna fix a leak."

"We've got a situation down here, Hubie. Help me out."

Ash tugged the small radio from his belt and held it with both hands. Its screen was lit a bright orange. It remained that way during a transmission and shortly afterward.

Abandoning his job and the town of Marlowe Bay weren't issues for Ash. Did he enjoy working as a porter? It was fine, he supposed. It certainly didn't fulfill him. Not much he did in the Witness Protection Program had that result.

Ash smirked as he stared at the radio. He'd never thought of any work as fulfilling. Why start now?

He flopped back on the bed and set the radio on his chest. Ash stared up at the concrete ceiling. A counselor in prison once told him stress resulted from knowing the right choice yet doing the opposite. Ash thought it was nonsense at the time. Now he thought maybe the counselor was onto something.

The radio came alive. "*Ash,*" Finley whispered now. "*Please report in. It's super important.*"

He lifted the radio to his lips and pressed the transmit button. "*Ash here.*"

"*Finally!*" Finley exclaimed. "*Where are you?*"

"*The basement.*"

"*Come to the main lobby.*"

"*What's going on?*"

"*The police are here.*"

Ash sat up. "*The cops?*" He instantly started to sweat (or some nervous, physical reaction).

"*They're looking for Ramon and asking about you. I've gotta go.*"

***

The basement ran the length of the hotel, allowing multiple access points to the main level. There were three stairwells. Two at opposite ends of the basement and one just around the corner from the main lobby. Even though there were two passenger elevators, only one went down to the basement.

Before leaving the maintenance area, Ash removed his cell phone from the small duffel underneath the bed. Considering recent events, it seemed prudent, especially with the police now in the hotel. He might need to make a hastier exit from Marlowe Bay than previously thought. Situations rarely went well for him when cops were involved.

Ash trotted north toward the stairwell in the middle of the hotel. He climbed the steps to the first floor, taking them two at a time, and stepped into the hallway.

Guests walked by. Some made their way to the lobby. Others proceeded north to the hotel's shops. It was possible some guests were headed toward one of the rear exits that would take them to the boardwalk and a visit to the beach.

Ash surveyed the crowd. His head swiveled back and forth as he looked for Daphne Winterbourne and Carrie Fenton. He didn't see either woman and felt clashing emotions—relief and disappointment. Relief that his presence wouldn't put Daphne into danger. Disappointment that he might not get to see her one more time.

That could change at any moment, he knew. It seemed a reality with the conferences. Attendees left the hotel only for meals since the hotel's main restaurant was under construction. However, its coffee shop and convenience store were still operating. Whenever a conference panel ended, the attendees wandered aimlessly back and forth through the main lobby. They were often in clumps, chatting happily away on whatever subject brought them together.

Ash rounded the corner to the lobby and stopped. A cop stood in front of the concierge desk. He wore a dark blue uniform, its long sleeves rolled up to his forearms. He was tall and black, with thick shoulders and bulging biceps. His hair was cut close to his scalp.

Sylvia Grayson stood next to the officer, spluttering and pointing at the notepad in his hands. Her dress was twisted once more, and her hair mussed again. Ash believed that must be the conference president's natural state.

A group of conference attendees formed a circle around the two. Estelle and Maxine huddled with three other women, each of them in the yellow T-shirts of the Mystery Mavens. Thelma Bennett stood with another group of women, each in their black Beautiful Bookworms' sweatshirts.

Ash caught the eye of Finley just as the front desk clerk pointed at him and shouted, "There he is!"

Those exact words hadn't been shouted in Ash's direction for some time. His first instinct was to turn and run. It was the action his former self—the one who'd been a Dawg—would have taken. In that life, it was always better to act first and think about it later. It could mean the difference between life and death.

However, Ash didn't run, even as every guest in the lobby looked in his direction. The children at the fountain stopped splashing in the water to witness his entrance. Ash pulled his shoulders back and lifted his chin. Although he really didn't know what was going on, he'd been in worse situations. No one was shooting at him now.

The cop lowered the notepad, and his bored eyes narrowed as he appraised the new arrival.

"That's him." Sylvia's voice echoed off the hotel's tile floor. "That's the porter. He'll know where to find Ramon."

"Sir," the officer said with a demanding wave, "come here."

Ash painted on a smile, an act he never did for a cop while he was with the Dawgs. The club's relationship with the law was entirely antagonistic. Showing any kindness to a police officer was tantamount to admitting weakness. However, he'd learned in his short time in the Witness Protection Program that most people responded well to a polite grin.

When he neared the officer, Ash could read the man's silver nametag—Greenway. His uniform was impeccable, and he smelled of sweet cologne.

"It's really that valuable?" Greenway asked Sylvia.

"Easily," she said.

"Is it insured?"

"Why would we do that? We're supposed to sell it on Saturday at our auction. The money goes to furthering the goals of the conference."

"All right," the cop said, then turned to study Ash. He seemed surprised Ash stood an inch or two taller than him. "You're a big fella, aren't you?"

Ash remained silent and tried to keep his smile from faltering.

The officer's eyes focused tighter, the way a kid might when examining an ant with a magnifying glass, right before burning the insect to death with the sun's rays. "Name?" he asked.

"Asher Reed."

Officer Greenway jotted Ash's name into his notebook. "You know Ramon Martinez?"

"He does," Sylvia said with an emphatic nod. "Ask him. He knows that dirty dog."

The cop raised an eyebrow at the conference president.

"Well?" she said, withering under the lawman's gaze. "He does."

"I work with Ramon," Ash said. He didn't add more because he'd yet to figure out what was going on.

Sylvia pointed at Ash. "He and Ramon looked pretty chummy together, I know that much."

"That true?" Officer Greenway asked. "You two friends?"

"We work together. That's it."

"Uh-huh." The cop sighed heavily, then jotted something in his notebook.

Ash took the opportunity to glance at the concierge room. The door to the storage area was open. He wondered if Knuckles might have found Ramon.

The children abandoned the water fountain to come and watch the interview. One girl pointed at the officer's gun. Ash speculated their parents had slunk off somewhere, letting the fountain act as a surrogate babysitter. He couldn't blame the adults but disliked them, nonetheless.

Members of the Mystery Mavens and the

Beautiful Bookworms moved in closer. They whispered conspiratorially among their different groups.

Officer Greenway crossed his arms, the notebook and pen disappearing behind a bicep. "Where is Ramon now?"

Sylvia imitated the cop's stance, arms crossed, impatient curiosity blazing in her eyes.

"I don't know where he is," Ash said.

"Any thoughts where he might have gone?" Greenway asked.

"Maybe he's talking with Nadine."

"Who?"

Sylvia's eyes widened, but she remained silent.

"The manager," Ash said. "Nadine Delacroix."

"Why isn't she up here?" Greenway glanced around. "Seems like a situation she'd want some say in."

"Maybe it was misplaced," Syliva said softly.

"Misplaced?" the officer asked. "You said it was stolen."

"It is!" Sylvia motioned at Ash. "He and Ramon took it!"

"Ma'am," Greenway said. "I'm trying to figure this out."

The conference president shook her head. "Here I thought Ramon was sweet. He really fooled me."

Ash held his hands up in mock surrender. "Before we go any further, can someone tell me what's going on?"

"Aren't you paying attention?" Sylvia cried

and pointed at the storage room. "The manuscript is missing, and Ramon stole it!"

The Mystery Mavens and the Beautiful Bookworms moved even closer. One of them excitedly blurted, "A robbery!"

"Are they starting the murder mystery already?" Estelle Enderby asked. "I thought that wasn't until tomorrow night."

"That's what I thought, too," Maxine said.

Thelma leaned toward the two Mavens. "Maybe it's a sneak peek at what's to come," she whispered. "You know, so they juice the participation, especially from the authors."

Estelle smirked. "That won't help. The writers never take part in any of the good stuff."

"Be nice," Maxine said. "They've got lots on their minds."

"Ease up, Pollyanna. You're getting sunshine in my eyes."

Maxine ignored her friend's slight, and her face brightened. "Wouldn't it be great if Vivienne Hart played with us? I bet she knows her way around this hotel, in and out."

Officer Greenway lifted his hands in the air. "Ladies, please. Give us some room."

The crowd moaned its collective disappointment, but every guest complied by shuffling a few steps back.

The cop turned his attention to Ash. "Did you see the—" He waved a hand as he searched for the word.

"Manuscript," Sylvia prompted. "He was in the office with Ramon. He had to have seen it."

Estelle turned to her friend and asked, "You think that's what they're offering up as the auction's big finale?"

"Pretty clever, if it is." Maxine shrugged. "Might even drive up the bidding."

"This *has* to be part of the murder mystery," Thelma said. She rubbed her hands excitedly as she scooted forward. "We're winning again this year."

"Not a chance," Estelle said as the rest of the crowd inched forward.

"Yeah," Ash said. "I saw it earlier." He immediately realized his mistake and tried to correct his blunder. "Although maybe it wasn't the manuscript you're talking about."

"Which is it?" Officer Greenway asked, his voice laced with apathy. It seemed obvious he thought there were more important tasks than searching for a missing manuscript. "Did you or did you not see it?"

"Oh, he's good," Estelle whispered as the conference attendees crept ever closer.

"Is he a paid actor?" Thelma asked.

Maxine eyed the cop. "I think he was in an episode of Criminal Minds."

"I only saw a box," Ash said.

"That's right." Sylvia snapped her fingers. "The manuscript was in a box," she said to the police officer. "I forgot to tell you." She mimed its size by gesturing with her hands. "A cardboard one about this big."

"You should be taking notes," Estelle said to Maxine.

Thelma looked at the other Bookworms. "Someone keep notes," she whispered.

Officer Greenway held up his hands. "Please, folks. Give us some space."

The crowd reluctantly moved back again, but Estelle and Thelma remained rooted in their spots. They exchanged competitive glances.

"You two," the cop said. "Last warning."

Estelle and Thelma both frowned and unwillingly took a half-step back.

Greenway's gaze returned to Ash. "Was anything written on the box?"

"No," Sylvia answered quickly. "Nothing except the shipping address."

"Ma'am," the officer said. "You need to give us some room, too. I need to speak with Mr. Reed without interruption."

"Yes, of course." Sylvia blushed. "I totally understand." She stepped back until she was part of the crowd.

The cop inhaled deeply, and his gaze swept over Ash once more. The lawman lingered on the ball of fire on the back of Ash's hand. Greenway wrote something in his notepad. Ash had a pretty good idea what it was.

"How'd you know the manuscript was in the box?" the cop asked.

Even if Ramon stole the manuscript, Ash hated to throw him under the bus. He wanted to be a better man for many reasons, and helping the cops accuse a friend of theft bothered him. Ash ratted out his old club to protect his grandmother. There was no one to protect today, so Ash continued to play coy. "I guessed."

"You guessed?" Officer Greenway's lips twisted with frustration. "What do you mean you guessed?"

Estelle whispered a little too loudly, "The porter's not very believable, is he? I've never liked him."

"He's sure got a suspicious quality about him," Maxine added. "I'll say that much. Not sure how he ended up on—"

Thelma shushed them. "I can't hear what's going on."

"It's the only thing that makes sense," Ash said to the cop. "You're asking about a manuscript, but I never saw anything like that. There was a small box on the storage room desk. That I did see. Two plus two, right?"

Greenway's lips twisted with disbelief. "You're a regular mathematician."

Ash eyed Sylvia. "How do you know the manuscript was stolen?"

"The concierge room was wide open, and the manuscript was gone."

"Well," Ash said, "maybe Ramon put it in the hotel's safe."

"I checked." Sylvia pointed at Finley. "He did, too."

"Ramon could be carrying it around," Ash suggested.

"Why would he do that?"

"You asked him to keep an eye on it."

"He wasn't carrying it earlier when I saw you

two. Why would he now?" Sylvia's gaze slid to Officer Greenway. "Plus he's not responded to any calls from the front desk. Therefore, it was stolen and he's on the run. Definitely."

Ash didn't mention Knuckles to either Sylvia or the cop. He still wasn't certain if Ramon might have taken the manuscript. It was valuable and Ramon had commented earlier about taking it when they were in the storage room. Ramon was also in financial trouble with a bookie named Mr. Leo.

Ash also recalled Nadine leaving the storage room with something heavy in her bag. He suspected she took it. If the manager did have the manuscript, it didn't explain Ramon's absence now.

"Well?" Sylvia asked. She put her hands on her hips. "Where's Ramon, smart guy? Tell me that. Go on."

"All right," Officer Greenway said. "I ask the questions." He lifted his chin toward the concierge room. "That's Ramon's office. Isn't that correct?"

"Technically," Ash said, "it's a storage room. We all go in it."

"Who's we?" Estelle asked loudly.

"The porters," Maxine said. "Probably. Don't you think?"

"Maybe's it's a conspiracy." Thelma rubbed her hands some more. "Wouldn't that be great? We've never had a conspiracy before. They're really upping the mystery game this year."

Maxine nudged Estelle. "We should ask

Vivienne Hart to join our team."

"We don't need her," Estelle said. "We can win this on our own."

Thelma clucked. "If you get an author, we want one."

Officer Greenway scowled at the crowd before asking Ash, "All the porters have access to the storage room?"

Ash inhaled deeply before answering. He knew where this questioning was headed but couldn't stop this train now that it was moving. "That's correct," he said. "We all have access."

"You all." The cop's eyes slanted. "How many other porters are working today?"

There it was, the question Ash dreaded. Maybe he should walk away now, simply turn and leave. Yet Greenway would insist they continue the conversation, perhaps even down at the station. Before Ash could determine the safest answer, Sylvia sunk him.

"He's the only porter working today," Sylvia said. "Ramon told me. The rest of them are out sick."

"Sick?" Thelma asked. "What happened?"

"Outbreak," Estelle Enderby said. "Flu."

"That's what the desk clerk said." Maxine nodded. "The whole lot of them."

Thelma crinkled her nose. "It's a little too convenient, don't you think?"

"How so?" Estelle asked.

"The flu reduces the pool of suspects." Thelma's eyes quickly enlarged. "Although maybe someone poisoned the staff to get them out of the way. Like in a Russian spy thriller!"

The others in the crowd murmured their support of Thelma's theory.

Officer Greenway stared at the assembled guests until most of them shuffled backward, then honed his gaze on Estelle, Maxine, and Thelma. The three women took another half-step back, bumping into their friends.

The cop's attention swung to Ash. "So, you're the only porter working today." It wasn't a question.

Ash reluctantly said, "That's right."

"He's guilty," Estelle said delightedly.

"He is?" Maxine asked.

"No, no." Thelma clucked. "They wouldn't make the mystery that simple. Something else has to happen so we can get involved. Otherwise, it's not a game; it's a play. Listen. It's coming."

Officer Greenway made an entry into his notebook. "Where were you?" he asked without looking up.

"When?" Ash turned his palms toward the ceiling. "I've been all over the hotel."

The cop's expression soured. "Where were you when the manuscript was stolen?"

"I don't know when it was stolen."

The cop rolled his eyes. "Don't play dumb."

"I don't think he's playing," Estelle said.

"If he is," Maxine added, "he's really good at it."

Thelma shushed them. "The reveal is coming, and I wanna hear it." She leaned forward with anticipation.

"Try this," Greenway said. "Where were you when the front desk clerk started calling for you?"

"In the basement." Ash pointed at the ground and immediately felt foolish for the gesture.

"What were you doing down there?"

"Maybe," Estelle said with an enthusiastic point at Ash, "he was hiding the manuscript."

"Oh, that's good," Maxine said. "We're definitely winning this year."

"I was taking a break." Ash could have been more detailed, but hedging always seemed natural when dealing with an inquiring cop.

The officer looked toward the hallway where the elevators were, then he looked in the opposite direction, which was where Ash had arrived from. "You didn't take an elevator?"

"Stairwell," Ash said.

"How many of them are there?"

"Three. Two at opposite ends of the building, one right around the corner."

"What about the security footage?" Greenway pointed at a camera mounted above the entrance, then one near the front desk. "Where's the security office?"

Ash shrugged. "There's no security office, and the cameras don't work. They're only a deterrent."

"So, no footage of anyone walking in or out of the hotel?"

"None."

"Nothing recording who goes in or out of the

concierge's room?"

"That's correct."

A murmur of disbelief rushed through the Mavens and the Bookworms. Sylvia Grayson threw her hands in the air, "Oh, that's great. I would never have left the manuscript with the concierge if I had known that."

Ash raised a questioning eyebrow toward her, recalling Ramon's statement that he warned her about the non-functioning cameras. The conference president looked away.

Greenway's gaze swept back and forth between the hallways. He looked as if he was deciding something. Finally, he said, "You stay here, where I can keep an eye on you until I sort out this mess."

"I never did trust that porter." Estelle shook her head. "Something seemed off about him."

"She's right." Maxine smiled at the others in her group. "Estelle and I never trusted that one."

Thelma frowned. "He seemed all right to me."

Chapter 6

Ash leaned an elbow on the concierge desk, his gaze swept back and forth.

Nearby, Officer Greenway interviewed Finley Hester. The desk clerk's face spasmed like he had an acute case of Tourette's syndrome. Finley made eye contact with Ash, then looked away when he answered whatever question the cop had asked.

The guests waiting to check in watched the officer and desk clerk with growing impatience. Several men with frustrated expressions threw their hands in the air. Their spouses reacted in a variety of ways. One patted her husband's arm and whispered soothing words. A second rolled her eyes and turned away. The third woman mirrored her husband's action and tossed her hands into the air, too.

A group of children returned to the fountain. They ran around it, dragging their hands through the water, and making motorboat sounds.

Overhead, a singer crooned about picking a plum from the tree of life.

Ash knew staying in the main lobby with the cop was asking to be seen by Daphne Winterbourne. If that happened, he would certainly talk with her, but his simple presence put her in jeopardy. It was something he never wanted to happen again.

A little girl near the fountain abruptly straightened and looked toward the north hallway. She hopped, pointed, and hollered, "Kitty!"

An orange cat stood at the edge of the lobby, surveying the activity.

"Travis?" Ash pushed off the desk to stand upright.

Another girl, roughly the same age as the first, shouted, "Meow meow!"

A bratty looking boy in obvious need of a time-out yelled, "Let's get 'im!"

The splashing in the fountain stopped as the children rushed toward Travis.

"Hey!" Ash barked. "Don't do that!"

None of the kids listened as they followed the bolting tom into the north hallway.

Ash pushed off the concierge desk and took two quick steps before the cop loudly said, "Stop!"

Officer Greenway glared at Ash. So did the Mystery Mavens and some members of the Beautiful Bookworms.

"Look at him," Estelle said. "Making a break for it."

Maxine turned toward her friend. "He wasn't very fast."

Ash searched for Travis, but the cat was gone.

Officer Greenway moved closer to Ash. Suspicion filled his eyes. "Now, what were you yelling about?"

"My cat," Ash said. He motioned toward the north hallway.

The cop glanced around. His hardened expression morphed into one of disbelief. "I don't see any cat."

"Someone must have let him out of his carrier," Ash said, "and he ran down that hallway."

"You think I'm dumb?" Greenway cocked his head. "Nobody brings a cat to work."

"That's not true," Thelma said. "Bookstores have kitties all the time."

"I know," Maxine said with an agreeable nod. "It's one of the reasons I insist on shopping in person."

"This ain't a bookstore, Maxie. The porter's telling stories." Estelle eyed Thelma. "Stop fraternizing with the enemy, will ya? We're at war."

"I'm staying here for a couple of days," Ash said. "There was a flood in my apartment, so I've got a rollaway in the basement. I'm keeping the cat in the storage room."

Greenway eyed Sylvia. "You see something like that when you visited the concierge?"

"Yeah," she said, elongating the word. It sounded like she was disappointed by proving Ash was right about something. Her face brightened, though, and she added, "The cat was there when I gave the manuscript to Ramon." She thumbed toward Ash. "So this one had extra incentive to go into the storage room."

"If someone let me," Thelma said, "I would

have brought my cat to work every day. Would have made work a lot more fun."

Maxine nodded. "How great would that be?"

Estelle nudged her friend with an elbow. "Pay attention, Maxie. The cat's a diversion." Estelle pointed at Ash. "This joker is trying to confuse us."

Greenway stepped closer. "The desk clerk reported you saw the manager. That right?"

"I already said that."

"Yeah, you said that all right." Greenway's brow furrowed. His gaze dropped to his notepad, but it didn't stay there long. Instead, his eyes popped up and settled on Ash. "The desk clerk didn't see the manager, though."

"He was busy," Ash said. "Checking in guests."

"What do you think that means?" Maxie asked.

Estelle flicked a hand in her direction. "Nothing. That desk clerk was so underwater he needed a life jacket. He wouldn't have seen a tugboat go by."

Thelma rubbed her chin. "I don't know," she said. "A missing manager seems important."

Officer Greenway's eyes cut toward the Mavens and Bookworms and their chattering stopped. He looked at Ash and asked, "Where was this manager when you saw her?"

"Is Nadine in trouble?" Ash didn't have any loyalty to Nadine, but helping the cops get answers to a problem he didn't quite understand seemed wrong. His desire to be a better man collided against his ingrained distrust of law enforcement.

The officer put his hands on his hips. Sylvia mimed his action.

"You say you saw the manager," Greenway said, "yet she's not here. No one else has seen her."

"Well," Ash said with some reluctance, "Ramon saw her."

"How?"

"She went into the storage room and talked with him."

"If that was her," Sylvia said, "I'm sure she had a good reason. She's dealing with an epidemic, after all."

The crowd rumbled and several words fluttered above the rest—outbreak, flu, and Robitussin.

Greenway leaned closer to Ash. "Are you saying the manager and the concierge worked together to steal the manuscript?"

"He's not saying that," Sylvia said quickly. She eyed Ash. "You're not saying that, are you?"

"No, that's not what I'm saying." Ash still didn't want to share his suspicion that Nadine carried something away from the room. "I don't know if anyone stole anything. All I'm saying is Nadine talked with Ramon."

Syliva waved her hands one over the other, the way a Vegas card dealer does when accepting cash. "See? Nadine isn't involved. Let's focus on the concierge." Her eyes darkened. "The dog."

"The manager always seemed nice to me," Estelle said.

"Me, too," Maxine added, "but it's the nice ones who always end up being the villain."

"Shush," Thelma said. "There's a clue in here. I'm sure of it."

Greenway pointed at the storage room. "Is that where you saw her?"

Ash grudgingly nodded. "I did."

"She had the manuscript with her?"

"I don't know." That was the truth. He didn't know if Nadine had the manuscript with her, only that her slouchy purse suddenly seemed heavy. That was an observation he kept to himself.

"Where'd she go?" Greenway asked.

Ash jerked his head toward the north hallway, the same way he'd come into the lobby.

"All right," the cop said. "Get back where you belong and don't even think about moving."

Ash resentfully returned to the concierge desk and resumed his leaning position. He pulled his cell phone from his pocket. It was time to call for help. He flipped it open and dialed two digits before Daphne Winterbourne ran into the main lobby from the north hallway. Her eyes were wide with fright.

On her heels was Carrie Fenton. Surprise also registered on her face.

"Call the police!" Daphne shouted.

"Nine one one," Carrie added.

Ash slipped his phone back into his pocket as others in the lobby pulled theirs out.

The assembled Mavens and Bookworms pointed at Officer Greenway.

Daphne hurried toward the cop with Carrie close behind. The crowd parted, allowing the two women in.

Ash lowered his gaze and nonchalantly tried to hide his face by bringing a hand up to his forehead.

"What's going on?" Greenway asked.

Out of breath, Daphne said, "There's a body."

"In the stairwell." Carrie pointed in the direction they'd just come from. "Just around the corner."

Daphne added, "He's dead."

"I told you it was a murder mystery," Estelle Enderby exclaimed. "Let's go!"

The Mystery Mavens and the Beautiful Bookworms started for the stairwell, hurrying away from Daphne and Carrie.

"Everybody stop!" Officer Greenway hollered, halting the conference attendees in their tracks. "Nobody move!" He pointed at Finley. "You, confirm the body. Don't touch anything. Report back."

"Yes, sir." The desk clerk ran off.

Greenway grabbed the microphone attached to his shoulder epaulet. He pressed the transmit button and announced his call sign.

A dispatcher's voice came through the small speaker. "*Go ahead.*"

The officer said, "Report of a body at my location. Need more units."

"*Copy.*"

Greenway's gaze snapped to Ash. Daphne and Carrie followed his eyes.

"Big fella," the cop said. "That's the same stairwell you took up from the basement. Right?"

Ash looked at the floor now, his hand still covering the side of his face. "Maybe."

"No maybes." Greenway bent to get Ash's attention. "It's time for the truth. Is it or is it not the same stairwell you came up?"

He nodded but didn't look at the officer. His hand still blocked his face.

"How did you come up that stairwell and not see a body?" the cop asked.

"It wasn't there."

"You came up from the basement. Had to be there."

Ash shrugged. "No one was in the stairwell when I came up."

Someone moved closer now. Ash could feel them standing there. His hand pressed harder against his forehead and he refused to look up. Fingers reached out and traced the fireball tattoo on the back of his hand.

"Brody?" Daphne looked at him stunned.

***

In his previous life as the Satan's Dawgs' bookkeeper, Ash knew many women. Some of them adored the patch on the back of his leather vest. Others were attracted to the aura of danger surrounding him. Those women came in various shapes, sizes, ages, and colors.

Yet they all had one thing in common: they didn't hold a place in Ash's heart.

He never held any lover dear. At least not the way the books in high school English class made out. Ash spent time with each of them, some longer than others. The relationships were mutually beneficial as he got something and the women got something. However, the words and feelings Ash shared in those moments were always hollow platitudes he could quickly distance himself from.

In the end, every woman moved on, either to other club members or to men with a different threat of risk. Their leaving didn't matter to Ash, since that was the life he'd sought as a younger man.

To the Dawgs, embracing tenderness with a woman was never done. Exposing any part of one's emotional underbelly was a good way to seed doubt among the other members, which eventually lead to getting beat out of the club. Ash never allowed himself to believe in anything more than transactional relationships.

That was until he met Daphne Winterbourne at The Red Herring, the only mystery bookstore in Pleasant Valley, Maine where he was first assigned by the program. He lowered his hand and stared into the eyes of the woman he'd thought about almost constantly since they met.

"My God." Daphne's eyes softened, and a smile crept across her face. "It's you."

"Welp," Carrie Fenton said with a smirk. "That's that."

Officer Greenway stepped away from Sylvia Grayson. "Who's Brody?"

Ash never looked away from Daphne.

"I can't believe it's really you." She reached out and touched Ash's hand again.

"You two know each other?" the cop asked.

"They're old friends," Carrie Fenton said.

"I see that." Greenway moved closer. "So is it Brody or Asher?"

The Mavens and the Bookworms gathered tighter around now.

Thelma said, "I don't understand what's happening. What did I miss?"

"Ugh," Estelle grunted. "They're making it a romantic mystery this year."

Maxine bumped her friend. "Don' be a grouch. I sort of like it."

Estelle's shoulders slumped. "There's no room for romance in a mystery."

"Janet Evanovich might disagree," Thelma said.

"So would Vivienne Hart," Maxine added. "She should really be here. I think she knows—"

Greenway snapped his fingers and held up a hand at the clustered readers. A murmur of disappointment spread through the crowd.

Ash and Daphne continued to stare at each other, ignoring everyone around them. Their eyes revealed the words neither spoke.

The cop tapped Ash's shoulder. "Answer my

question, big fella. Brody or Ash?"

Ash blinked and looked at the cop. "Ash."

"Brody is a pet name," Daphne said. Her eyes remained on Ash.

Greenway cocked his head. "Explain how that works."

Neither Ash nor Daphne had to clarify anything since Finley Hester sprinted into the lobby then. He ran directly to Officer Greenway, his shoes slapping on the tile. When he stopped, Finley's face spasmed with uncontrolled energy. He repeatedly thumbed in the direction of the stairwell. "The body."

"You confirmed it?" Greenway asked.

The desk clerk nodded. "It's Ramon." He inhaled deeply before announcing. "He's dead."

Chapter 7

"You're with me," Officer Greenway said to Ash. "I'm not letting you out of my sight."

"What'd I do?"

"What do you think?"

Ash had admitted to being in the office with Ramon while the manuscript was in there. The cop knew only the concierge and the porters had access to the storage room. The manuscript was missing, and Ramon turned up dead. Worse, Ash had admitted to being in the middle stairwell only minutes before Ramon's body was discovered. There was only one thing to think— Ash was the number one suspect now.

Greenway grabbed Ash's elbow and tugged him in the direction of the stairwell.

Daphne started to follow, but the cop held up a hand. "Just him." He looked at the crowd. "All of you, stay here."

"Typical," Estelle said. "Control the flow of information."

Thelma nodded in agreement. "Makes it harder to solve the mystery."

Maxine leaned toward her friend. "You think maybe this is real?"

"Who murders someone at a mystery convention?" Estelle clucked. "We're all crime-solving experts here. This is what we do."

"Some faster than others," Thelma said with a mischievous twinkle in her eye.

"Ugh," Estelle muttered. "Bookworms."

Concern washed over Daphne's face as she watched Ash.

"It's okay," he said. "I'll find you when we're done."

Carrie Fenton put her hand on Daphne's shoulder. "You'll see him again."

"Bah," Estelle Enderby said, louder than necessary. "Romance." She blew a raspberry.

Officer Greenway pulled Ash's arm. "Let's go."

The two headed toward the north hallway. The children at the fountain waved at the policeman as he and Ash passed by.

Around the corner, a small group of guests gathered at the open stairwell.

"Make way," Greenway commanded.

The looky-loos separated, creating a pathway for the cop and Ash.

Just inside the stairwell door, Ramon Martinez lay face down on the concrete floor. A pool of blood spread out from a wound on the back of his head. The steps to the upper floors were behind Ramon. Stairs to the basement were to the right.

The officer turned to the crowd. "Everybody back. Nothing to see here."

Whispers of disagreement rose through the onlookers as they hesitantly shuffled away.

Greenway eyed Ash. "Don't move." The cop pushed him against the opened door. "Not one word."

Ash lifted his hands in surrender. He didn't need the officer's admonishment to stay quiet. He'd been in situations like this before, both with the Dawgs and since his entry into the Witness Protection Program. The best course of action was always to remain quiet. Anything he said could and would be used against him in a court of law, and he'd already said too much about Ramon and Nadine.

The officer stepped closer to the body and squatted. His leather duty belt creaked as he did so. Greenway pressed two fingers against the side of Ramon's neck. A few seconds passed before the cop stood. He grabbed his shoulder microphone, pressed the transmit button, and announced his call sign. The officer then said, "Body confirmed. Alert a supervisor."

"*Copy*," a dispatcher responded.

Greenway looked up the stairwell, then leaned over and looked down. His face hardened when he turned back. "This is the way you came up from the basement?"

Ash thought about lying, but he'd already cornered himself with his earlier admission. Lying would only make it worse, especially if he was caught doing so. Ash nodded once.

"How'd Ramon act when he saw you?"

"When?"

"When you came up from the basement." Greenway pointed down the stairs.

"He wasn't here. In fact, no one was in the stairwell when I came up."

"You sure?"

"Why would I lie about that?" There were plenty of reasons, but it was best to play dumb. "Maybe Ramon was on an upper floor and coming down," Ash said. "I didn't bother to check."

"Don't you feel bad?" Greenway motioned at the body. "That's your friend."

"I know," Ash said. "It doesn't change the fact Ramon wasn't here when I came up."

The officer squatted near the body again. His leather gear creaking once more. He pointed at a deep wound on the back of the concierge's head. "What do you make of it?"

Ash leaned to get a better look. The injury to Ramon's skull looked deep, as if it might have been caused by a heavy object.

"What do you think caused that, big fella? Maybe a hammer?"

Ash shrugged. The wound looked as if it might have been caused by such a tool, but he couldn't be sure. He didn't want to guess and be right. Doing so could let the cop believe he was involved somehow.

Greenway stood. He stepped over the body and made a big show of looking down the stairwell. "Why don't you guess what's lying on the landing below?"

Ash didn't have to speculate. He knew from the cop's actions.

"It's a hammer," Greenway said. "Wanna bet we find your fingerprints on it?"

"Not a chance," Ash said as confidently as he could. "Won't happen."

Something metallic fell in the basement, and the sound reverberated up the stairwell.

Greenway moved toward the wall to get a better angle. Even from where Ash stood, he knew the cop couldn't see into the basement. The landing was as far as he could see and only halfway to the bottom floor.

"Who's there?" the cop shouted.

Footsteps faded away.

Greenway glanced at Ash. "Stay here," he said and hurried down the steps. He took them two at a time and made a racket that echoed through the stairwell.

Ash took another look at Ramon, then stepped away from the door, letting it close behind him.

***

Ash pulled his cell phone from his pocket and reluctantly dialed a number he memorized. He was about to call the marshals when Daphne Winterbourne had sprinted into the lobby a few minutes earlier. He should have continued with the action, but it might have stopped him from interacting with her.

His presence might cause her danger if anyone connected to his past saw them together. It was unlikely to happen again, but a lot of unlikely events had occurred in the past few months.

Calling this number didn't feel good, but it was a mature action, the right choice, so to speak. Convincing himself of that was going to take Ash some time.

The phone rang once and was quickly answered.

"Big Dog Plumbing," a woman answered in a monotone voice. "We're off the leash and ready to bite into your clog."

The marshals had created a hotline for Ash to use in the event an emergency arose. It was always under the guise of a business. That was done for safety reasons in case someone hostile was listening to the call. In the past, the cover businesses had been a travel agency, a horoscope hotline, and a seafood warehouse.

Ash learned a few weeks ago that everyone in the Witness Protection Program had a number like this. He also discovered he might be the only one to ever call in more than once.

He said to the operator, "I need to schedule some service." Two words in that statement, schedule and service, amounted to a countersign Marshal Krumland insisted he learn. Ash never needed a password before, but his witness inspector said it was to add a new level of security.

"Hello, Mr. Reed," the operator said. "We are here to help." The woman's voice remained so flat and detached Ash thought she might be a robot until he heard a keyboard clacking in the background.

Ash remembered one of the girls that hung around the Satan's Dawgs. She was attractive but devoid of personality. She had a flat voice, much like the operator, and would drone on whenever she drank alcohol. Ash avoided her as much as possible. Unfortunately, he had to stay on the line if he hoped to get some help.

"This call is being recorded for quality assurance," the operator said. "Is there an emergency situation?"

"You can say that."

"I did not understand that response. Please say yes or no."

Ash pulled the phone from his ear and considered it. Was the marshal service using a computer to answer the emergency line? If so, why was there keyboard clacking? Was it meant to add a sense of calming realism? Was this digitized controller the outcome of his many hotline alerts, or was this a result of some of the poor interactions he'd had with previous operators?

Before Ash could address any of his internal questions, the stairwell door burst open. Officer Greenway, his face twisted in fury, stepped into the hall. He briefly stiffened when he saw Ash with a cell phone to his ear.

The officer hurried over. "Who you calling?"

"A plumber."

The operator's response droned in Asher's ear. "All of our plumbers are in the field right now. If you are experiencing an emergency, please hang up and contact local authorities."

Greenway stepped forward and put his nose awfully close to Ash's. "Hang up," he said.

"Hanging up," the operator droned in Ash's

ear. "Have a nice day." The call ended.

Ash lowered the phone and snapped it close.

"Tell me, big fella," Officer Greenway said, "why do you need a plumber right now?"

Ash shrugged, trying to come up with a plausible story, but nothing came to him. "We have a leak," he said, "on the third floor."

Greenway held out his hand. "Gimme the phone."

"Am I under arrest?"

"You're suspect number one." The officer snapped his fingers. "The phone."

"What about the person in the basement?" Ash asked. "The one who ran from you."

"I don't even know if there was a person." Greenway waggled his fingers. "The phone."

"We heard footsteps."

"Maybe it was your accomplice." Greenway snapped his fingers a second time.

"I don't have an accomplice."

"So, you're admitting you did this on your own? Thank you."

Ash stopped talking then. He was tired of digging himself deeper into a hole.

"Listen, big fella." Greenway scowled. "Either you gimme the phone now, or I'm gonna take it from you and slap the handcuffs on until we figure everything out."

"When you put it that way." Ash handed the cell phone to the cop. He wasn't worried about his true identity being discovered since no information was stored in the burner. The device's history would show only one number—

the one he had just called. If Greenway decided to dial it himself, he wouldn't learn more than Big Dog Plumbing had a computerized operator.

Several patrol officers, two men and one woman, trotted around the corner. The female cop said, "The detective is right behind us."

Greenway nodded, then pointed at the stairwell door. "One of you secure that area. The rest of you lock down the lobby. I've got the big fella here." Greenway grabbed Ash's elbow. "Let's take a walk. I'm sure the detective will want to talk with you."

***

A well-dressed man with perfectly combed salt and pepper hair entered the hotel lobby, took a few steps, and stopped. He wore a dark blue suit, pink shirt, and a printed tie. His eyes swept over the assembled crowd.

The officers in the lobby stopped whatever they were doing and looked at the new arrival. Each offered some type of friendly gesture toward the detective—a nod, a wave, or a lift of their chins.

"Detective Landry caught the case," Greenway said under his breath. "You're in for it now."

The investigator noticed a uniformed cop standing outside the concierge's office. Landry walked over and peered into the room. The two lawmen exchanged some words. Landry looked toward the ceiling before considering the storage room once again.

Ash would have liked a peek in there, too. He wanted to know how Travis got out of his cage. Ramon certainly wouldn't have let the cat out. Had the tom figured out how to escape on his own? Or had Knuckles found Ramon in the concierge room and let the cat out for spite? It seemed like something the thug would do.

Greenway lifted his chin in the direction of the detective. "Landry is like an alligator," he said. "He bites into a lying suspect, drags them into the depths of the truth, and twists them around until they don't know which way is up."

"Sounds like a nice guy."

"You'll find out soon enough."

The radio on Ash's hip beeped. *"Hubie,"* Finley Hester said through the microphone. *"Please report to the lobby."*

A uniformed policewoman stood behind the front desk, talking with Finley. He shook his head and shrugged, a clear indication he had no idea where the hotel's maintenance man was.

"Squelch that noise," Greenway said, "and give it to me."

Ash silenced the radio, then handed it to Greenway.

"No lip this time?" the officer asked. "We're making progress."

Detective Landry stepped away from the concierge room, his gaze taking in everyone gathered in the lobby. His attention landed on Ash and Officer Greenway. He lifted a finger in the air, then walked toward the edge of the lobby. The man disappeared around the corner.

"You know," Ash said, "I had nothing to do with Ramon's death."

"Save your breath." Greenway smirked. "You're gonna need it."

Carrie Fenton and Daphne Winterbourne stood nearby. Greenway insisted they stay close since the detective would want to speak with them about discovering the body. Daphne waved surreptitiously at Ash. He smiled and mirrored her gesture.

Members of the Bookworms and the Mavens gathered around Sylvia Grayson at the lobby's south edge, closest to the elevators. Her dress remained twisted around her waist and her hands were buried in her hair.

Ash couldn't hear everything Sylvia said, but did hear the words, "Opening ceremony." She animatedly pointed toward the conference center. Her suggestion was thoroughly ignored, though, when the Mavens and the Bookworms moved in the opposite direction, toward the center stairwell and lifeless concierge. Sylvia took a final glance toward the conference center, then hurried toward Ash and Greenway.

As Thelma Bennett passed Ash, she winked at him and Maxine Coleman offered a polite wave.

Estelle Enderby clucked and said, "The conference is starting to take a turn for the better."

"This day couldn't get any worse!" Sylvia said when she neared Officer Greenway. "How much longer is this going to take?"

"It's a homicide scene," the cop said. "It's going to take hours."

"I know, I know." Her voice rose in a hysterical whine. "The conference is ruined. We're going to have to cancel the opening ceremony."

"Ma'am," Greenway repeated.

"The hotel doesn't even have our food ready." She turned to Ash. "Only one cook is in the kitchen. He hasn't even made any snacks."

"Step back," the officer said.

Sylvia ignored the request, her attention still on Ash. "Where's Nadine? She's not answering my calls. I really need to speak with her."

Ash was about to answer, but Greenway cut him off.

"Walk away," the officer told Sylvia. "You're interfering with a murder investigation."

"How could this be happening?" Sylvia asked. She shoved her hands into her hair and walked away turning in circles as she went. The conference president was a spinning top set loose across the hotel floor.

The line for the registration desk was down to a single person. Finley banged away on his keyboard as the waiting guest frequently glanced at the police activity occurring behind him.

In the center of the main lobby, the winged cherub continued to drool water into the fountain's pool. All the children were gone, likely dismissed by a uniformed officer. If only one good thing came from the day's events, Ash would point to that.

Detective Landry appeared at the north edge of the lobby. He paused, obviously studying everything from a new angle. When he moved, the assembled mystery fans spread apart, creating a lane for him to reach Officer Greenway and his detainee.

Estelle Enderby asked loudly, "How was the concierge killed?"

Landry dismissed her with a wave as he passed by.

"Rude," Maxine Coleman said.

"As a burp in church," Thelma Bennett added.

"Let's follow him," Estelle said.

The detective spun on his heel. He waggled his hand at the three women. "If any of you get within three feet of me, I'll arrest you for interfering with a police investigation." He gestured to the rest of the Mavens and Bookworms. "That goes for you, too."

Maxine inhaled sharply. "That's not how this game is played."

Estelle bumped her friend with an elbow. "It's not a game, Maxie."

"If it was," Thelma said, "there'd be a friendly cop who shared information with us."

Landry snapped his fingers and pointed. "Not another word, ladies." He motioned to the rest of the assembled women. "From any of you."

Estelle huffed and turned around. She headed toward the north corridor. The remaining members of the two book clubs took similar action, huffing once before falling in behind Estelle. It resembled a gray-haired train leaving the station.

Landry spun, clapped his hands one time, and said, "Where were we?" He resumed his course toward Officer Greenway and Ash. When he arrived at them, he nodded at the uniformed cop. "Greenie."

"Detective Landry. You see the body?"

"I did. An awful mess."

"You find the hammer?" Greenway's question was loaded with extra concern.

"What about it?"

The officer turned his head and whispered, but Ash clearly heard, "There was no blood."

Landry shrugged. "Don't worry. The CSI team will find an explanation for it." He turned toward Ash. "This the guy?"

"Yeah," Greenway said. "He won't admit to anything, though."

"He will." Detective Landry crossed his arms as he studied Ash. "They all do. Eventually." His lips twisted, and he scrunched his nose while his gaze slowly traveled Ash's length. "What's his name?"

Since the question wasn't asked of him, Ash remained silent. He kept his expression flat, a skill he'd learned with the Dawgs and perfected during his time behind bars.

"Asher Reed," Greenway said.

Landry scoffed. "Doesn't look like an Asher."

"Funny you say that. Another guest called

him Brody." The cop motioned toward Daphne.

"I can see that." Landry nodded. "*Brody*. Sounds like some high school jock whose glory days are behind him."

Greenway chuckled. "You've got this one pegged."

The detective's eyes cut to Daphne. "What's that make her? The prom queen? What else did she say?"

"Claimed Brody was a pet name."

"Ridiculous," Landry said. "Pet name for what? She's covering for him."

"Maybe." Greenway shrugged a single shoulder. "She seemed surprised to see him. Like she didn't know he was supposed to be here."

"Probably an act to throw us off the scent." Landry's brow furrowed. "How'd this one and the guest know each other?"

"Supposedly they're old friends."

"That's not really an answer, is it?" Landry's attention returned to Ash. "Who's she with, Greenie?"

Greenway motioned to Carrie Fenton. "A third wheel."

"This keeps getting better," Landry said. "Three peas in a pod. Keep 'em separated, all right? We don't want them getting their stories straight."

Ash's expression tightened, but he quickly forced it back into an apathetic stare.

Once again, Daphne was pulled into a situation because of his background. Although, this background was fictional, courtesy of the U.S. Marshals. He didn't want Carrie Fenton talking with the law either. She knew more about his situation than almost anyone. She was the first person to discover he was hiding under an assumed name.

"You two," Greenway said, pointing to Daphne and Carrie. "Move apart. No talking."

Landry moved closer to Ash. Even though the investigator was almost nose to nose with Ash, he still directed his questions toward the nearby officer. "What's his middle name?"

"Big fella doesn't have one," Greenway said.

"That so?" The detective clicked his teeth together before muttering, "Asher No Middle Name Reed with a nickname of Brody." He glanced at Greenway. "You ran him through the system?"

"Came back clean," Greenway said.

The detective cocked his head. "Nothing?"

"Some traffic violations." The officer turned his palms up. "Nothing else."

"Tickets?" Landry gnawed on his lower lip as he reconsidered Ash once more. "What kind?"

"Speeding. Three times."

A sly smile spread across the detective's lips. "We got ourselves a lead foot. I guess that's something. A willful disregard for the law."

The police had interviewed Ash many times in his life. Even the FBI put him under the microscope. All those investigators directed their questions at Ash. This technique of directing questions away from him was something new, but Ash didn't let it affect his outward disposition. His thoughts and subsequent concerns remained hidden behind a mask of indifference.

Landry clicked his teeth together several times before asking, "What's Asher's job here at the hotel?"

"Man's a porter."

The detective looked away from Ash. His gaze bounced around the hotel lobby. He even turned a complete circle. "Where are the others?"

"Others, sir?" Greenway asked.

"The other porters. The other desk clerks. You'd think a dead man in a stairwell should result in a call for all hands on deck."

"There was an outbreak."

Landry's upper lip curled. "Outbreak of what?"

"The flu," Greenway said. "Most everyone is out."

"The manager?"

"Sick, too." The uniformed officer thumbed toward Ash. "Although this one claims he saw her earlier."

"Where?"

"Talking with our victim."

The detective's eyes narrowed. "Anyone else see the manager?"

"Haven't found anyone yet."

"Isn't that a fine kettle of fish?" The detective dragged his thumb across his chin. "A man ends up dead in a back stairwell after a rare manuscript was stolen. All made possible due to an outbreak of the flu. You know what I hate, Greenway?"

The officer looked at his shoes while he thought. When he landed on something, Greenway lifted his head. "Coincidences?"

"Coincidences," Landry parroted. "That's right. Coincidences are fancy lies, confusing us about the truth." The investigator's attention settled on Ash's ball of fire tattoo. "When you ran this one's name, did any tattoos show up in the report?"

"None that I noticed. He didn't have a criminal record, so it's unlikely anyone would have ever made note of them."

"Just traffic infractions," Landry muttered with a slow, disbelieving nod. "Where's this guy live?"

As the detective continued to ask Greenway the questions, Ash retained an air of coolness. However, that's not what he felt inside. Landry bugged him. Ash wanted the opportunity to defend himself, but he wouldn't address the investigator first.

Landry contrived a power struggle with Ash by refusing to address any questions toward him. If he wanted to end the charade, Ash would have to do it some other way. Attacking the detective would certainly stop this act. It wouldn't have to be anything overly physical, just a simple push in the chest would suffice. However, shoving a cop was still an assault— Ash had been arrested for it before.

No, he needed something passive aggressive,

a move all cops hated. Ash shoved his fists into his pants pockets.

Landry moved a half step back and turned his body slightly to move his gun side away from Ash. Greenway performed the same action as if they were part of a synchronized dance team. They both pointed at Ash and together said, "Get your hands outta your pockets."

A sly smile formed on Ash's lips. "Jinx."

The detective smirked. "Get those meat hooks out of your pockets before we pull them out."

Ash leisurely pulled his hands from his pants and opened his palms to reveal he held nothing. While with the club, every interaction Ash ever had with law enforcement officers resulted in one of them ordering Ash to keep his hands out of his pockets. He didn't bother hiding his growing smile.

"Look at you," Landry said, his eyes narrowing with deepening suspicion. "Finally caught my attention. Hope you're happy."

"Not really."

"Guess you must have had trouble with the law before."

"I watch a lot of TV," Ash lied.

"Uh-huh." The detective frowned as his body relaxed. "You can answer my question, then. Where do you live?"

Ash told him.

Officer Greenway nodded. "That's what his driver's license says, too."

Landry pushed his tongue under his lower lip. "Walking distance from here."

Ash shrugged. "It's good for my heart."

The detective scoffed. "Good for your—" He eyed Greenway. "You believe this guy?" Landry's eyes cut back to Ash. "Mind if we search your apartment?"

"I've been here all day."

"That wasn't an answer."

"Feel free," Ash said, "but there was a flood."

The detective raised an eyebrow.

"From the unit above mine. I don't have access to it right now."

"Where are you staying then?"

"The basement."

"Of the hotel?"

Ash nodded. "For a few days until my landlord gets it cleaned up."

"You got a cot in the basement or something?"

"A rollaway."

"That so?" Landry rubbed his chin again. "Why didn't the hotel give you a room?"

"We're booked full for the mystery convention."

"Let me get this straight." Landry crossed his arms. "A flu outbreak happens at the same time your apartment is flooded and there are no rooms available."

"Coincidence," Officer Greenway said.

"Coincidence," Landry echoed. "Making it possible for you to be in the hotel beyond your regular shift with a less than proper number of staff."

"You're twisting the facts," Ash said.

The detective continued. "A valuable

manuscript goes missing even though it was being guarded by the concierge.”

“He wasn’t guarding it.” Ash immediately regretted speaking.

“Wasn’t guarding it, huh?” Landry asked. “What was the concierge doing with it, then?”

Ash waved his hand. “We’re off course here.”

“Feels like I’m on the right track. Greenie?”

The uniformed cop nodded. “You’re definitely on the right track.”

“Let’s add it up,” Landry said. The detective lifted a single finger. “Outbreak.” He raised another digit. “Apartment flood.” Landry continued to raise fingers as he rattled off his list. “Stolen manuscript. Murdered concierge. Porters can move freely about a hotel with impunity. How many is that?”

The detective held his hand in front of Ash’s face.

“Five,” Greenway said.

“I was asking him.” Landry lowered his hand. “That’s what we call in the business a preponderance of evidence.”

Ash crossed his arms. “Conviction requires beyond a reasonable doubt.”

“You’re a lawyer now? Practicing law while schlepping bags, huh? That’s a new one.” The detective’s expression darkened. “You know what I think? I think you found out about the manuscript and murdered the concierge for it. Then you ran home to your apartment and hid it. How’s that for staying on track?”

“Ramon was my friend,” Ash said. “I didn’t kill

him, and I certainly didn't take the manuscript back to my apartment. The flood, remember?"

"So you say." Landry's lips twisted. "We'll get a uniform to check out that claim. Although maybe you put it in your car, and that's why you don't care if we check your apartment. Where's your car?"

Ash stared at him.

"Don't tell me. I'll ask the desk clerk where the employees park. We'll find it eventually."

"I don't have a car," Ash said.

"No car?" The detective's voice rose with excitement, as if he just broke the case wide open. Landry grinned as he watched Ash. One second passed, then another, and finally a third. Finally, Landry said, "Three speeding tickets. Isn't that right, Greenway? Old lead foot here had three speeding tickets?"

"That's right."

"Tell me, Asher No Middle Name, how'd you get that many moving violations with no ride?"

Ash stared straight ahead. The cops could run his name through the Department of Licensing to find out if any vehicles were ever registered to him in the state of Georgia. They could do the same for any other state. The only vehicle ever registered to Ash was a motorcycle in Arizona, and that was under his real name. He needed to come up with a plausible answer as to the tickets and lack of transportation.

"I borrowed the car."

"Oh, yeah?" The detective grinned. "What kind of car?"

Ash knew the history Marshal Krumland had prepared for this alias. It was easy to remember: five years in the Army, a ten-year stint working in a restaurant kitchen, then the porter job. The marshal went light on the criminal history, though, and only gave Ash a handful of speeding tickets.

The location and dates of the infractions were included in Ash's preparation file. However, nothing was mentioned about the type of vehicle.

"No answer?" Landry asked.

"I don't remember."

"I'll give you that," the detective said. "I'm not a car guy myself. Surely, you can tell me who owned the car, the one you borrowed?"

Ash kept his expression flat. He couldn't provide a name the detective could easily disprove. It would make him look more guilty. If he uttered a fake name, the cops could refute that, too. Ash had dug himself into a hole. The best thing to do was stop digging.

"You didn't steal it," Landry said. He motioned to the nearby officer. "I believe that much. Any cop running the registration would know it was stolen. Greenway would have seen that in your record."

Ash remained silent.

"Well?" Landry said. "Who'd you borrow the car from?"

Several seconds passed before he finally said, "I don't remember."

"You got three speeding tickets in a car you

can't recall and owned by someone you don't remember." Landry leaned in and studied Ash. "There's something fishy about you."

Ash shrugged. "Guess I'm forgetful."

"Forgetful. That's it." Landry held his hand out. "Mind if we have your house keys?"

There was no reason not to give the detective what he wanted. If the investigator requested a search warrant, he'd get one. Ash knew how tight judges and cops were. The legal system never worked in his favor.

He pulled out the single key he carried and handed it to the detective. Landry stared at it.

"One key?"

"My apartment."

"Uh-huh." Landry straightened. "Tell you what, big guy. You wait right here while Officer Greenway reruns you through the computer."

"Sir?" the cop asked.

"Don't run him by his name." The detective pointed at the back of Ash's hand. "Start with the tattoo on the back of his hand. Look for anyone in the system that matches."

"You're crazy," Ash said half-heartedly.

"Like a fox." Landry snapped his fingers and eyed the uniformed officer. "Also, look for any intersections with that tattoo and the name Brody."

"Will do," Greenway said.

"We'll get to the truth of this," Landry said. "One way or another." He turned and headed toward the stairwell, stopping only to take Daphne and Carrie with him.

Chapter 8

Ash sat on the edge of the fountain and listened to the pitter-patter of a concrete angel dribbling saliva into the pool. Officer Greenway told him to sit there and not move while he conversed with the other officers. Ash looked toward the north hallway, where several cops stood now, and the last place he'd seen Travis.

Nearby, a boy roughly six years of age patted the fountain's water with both hands, creating an awkward drum beat to accompany the winged cherub's trumpet. Ash thought he might have been one of the children who chased after his cat. Right now, he was the only kid to have returned to the fountain.

"Rain, rain," the boy said, slapping the pool twice. "Go away." He smacked the water in time with each word.

"Hey, kid," Ash said under his breath.

The boy stopped singing and looked questioningly in Ash's direction. His fingers wriggled in and out of the pool.

"Where did that cat go?"

"It ran away," the kid said, smacking the water in rhythm with his words.

"Yeah, but where?"

"It. Ran. Away." The boy hit the water harder this time. Each word causing a splash on to the fountain's lip near Ash.

"Do me a favor," he said and leaned closer to the child. "Go tell your mother she wants you."

The boy glanced around. "What does she want?"

"You."

"I didn't do nothing."

"Make sure you tell her that."

The boy wandered off, water dripping from his hands onto the tile floor.

Ash leaned back to see if he could get a view into the north corridor. He couldn't. All he could see was a crowd gathered at the mouth of the hallway. Some Mystery Mavens and Beautiful Bookworms were there, but he couldn't see Daphne or Carrie. He sighed and turned his attention to the lobby.

A cop remained on guard outside the concierge room, likely waiting for an evidence team to process it. Ash really wanted to get a look at the room. He wasn't sure he'd find anything linked to the manuscript's theft or Ramon's murder, but he really wanted to know how Travis got out of his carrier.

Ash's gaze continued around the lobby, taking in the various onlookers. Standing at the edge of the lobby's south edge, nearest the elevators, was the author, Vivienne Hart. She was hard to miss with her long blond hair and tight red dress. She took in the whole spectacle the way a moviegoer might enjoy a blockbuster—brow furrowed, jaw set, darting eyes. Perhaps the intense demeanor was an author trait, witnessing every event as if it were potential fodder for a book.

When her gaze landed on Ash, their eyes met. Her head canted in a questioning manner. She took a tentative step toward him but suddenly stopped.

Finley Hester dropped onto the fountain's lip. He didn't settle next to Ash, but close enough where the two men could talk without shouting. Ash glanced at the front desk. For the moment, no one waited to check in. He turned his attention back to the south entrance, but Vivienne Hart was gone.

"How you doing?" the desk clerk asked. He chuckled. "Probably a stupid question."

"Have you seen my cat?"

"The one you put in the storage room?"

"He's running around the hotel now."

"That's gotta be a health code violation." Finley cocked his head. "Does he usually break out of his carrier?"

"Never done it before."

"The great escape artist."

"Yeah," Ash muttered.

"Things keep getting better, huh?"

"I wouldn't say that."

Finley glanced around the lobby, then slid closer to Ash. "Is this too close?"

"We might draw attention."

"Right, of course." Finley's right eye twitched, but he didn't move away. "I didn't want to say this too loud."

"Say what?"

"You and Ramon were friends, right?"

"Work friends, yeah." Not wanting to attract attention from the assembled police, Ash slid slightly away from the desk clerk. He also didn't look directly at Finley. It was how Ash learned to communicate in prison.

"Work friends like me and you?" A nervous smile appeared at the corner of Finley's lips. "You think we're friends, right?"

Ash nodded but remained silent. He continued to scan the lobby.

Nadine Delacroix hadn't come back to the lobby yet. Ash thought it was suspicious that an employee was murdered, and she wasn't front and center interacting with the police. Maybe Nadine had come in only for a moment, did whatever she had to do, then left. Nadine was supposed to be sick, after all. Was stealing the manuscript her reason for coming into the hotel while ill?

Also, Knuckles hadn't reappeared. Ash hadn't seen the tough guy since their initial conversation. Perhaps he was involved in Ramon's murder, but Ash had his doubts. Before he could consider it, Finley interrupted his thoughts.

"I appreciate that," the desk clerk said. "I think of us as friends, too." His eyes narrowed, and he made sure no one was listening before he leaned toward Ash. "I've got a question."

"Sit up straight," Ash said, not looking in the desk clerk's direction.

"Huh?"

"You're gonna attract attention."

"Right," the desk clerk said. He straightened and tried to look as unsuspicious as possible. His flickering smile didn't help. "Of course."

Ash cast a sideways glance at Finley. "Relax and ask your question."

Finley leaned forward and rested his elbows on his knees. "Why'd that woman call you Skeeter?"

"It's a nickname."

"A nickname?" Finley stiffened. "How's something like that come about?

Ash couldn't come up with a story fast enough, so he said, "You know how it is."

"You two are close?" Finley asked.

"We're friends."

"Isn't she one of the authors?"

Ash nodded.

"Where'd you meet?"

"In a bookstore."

"Around here?"

"Elsewhere."

"Huh." Finley's brow furrowed. "Pretty crazy you two running into each other here."

"Small world."

"That's what they say, but I've never been anywhere but here." Finley eyed the officer standing in front of the concierge room. He then leaned back and looked toward the north. He whispered, "The cops think you murdered Ramon."

"If they were sure of that, I'd be in handcuffs."

"You didn't, right?"

Ash nodded. "That's right."

Finley tittered. "That's what I said. The exact same thing. You didn't because you two were friends and all." The desk clerk's nervous giggling stopped. "Not sure that matters. The cops will prove what they wanna prove. If they don't have the evidence, they'll make it up."

It seemed a strange argument from Finley. Ash would never have suspected the man would have a poor opinion of law enforcement. However, he didn't argue with the desk clerk's assessment.

As far as Ash was concerned, the justice system was a stacked deck, and he was one of the many suckers waiting to be dealt another losing hand. It was an outlook he'd had since high school and became worse with his time in the Dawgs. The feeling decreased a little over the past few months with his interaction with a few officials concerned with his well-being.

Ash developed a sort of affinity toward his previous two marshals. One took a bullet for him while in California. Another rescued Ash from the club after they chased him into Oregon. He doubted he'd ever look at Lester Krumland the same way, but stranger things had happened to Ash recently.

He even established a grudging respect for the FBI agent who initially arrested him. That man found Ash's weak point, his love for his grandmother, and used it against him. Ash first believed he would never forgive the G-man, especially as thoughts of revenge coursed through his veins.

The longer he'd been away from the club, the more Ash realized life was different for the general population. Most citizens didn't fear the cops. They also weren't afraid of those they called brothers, like Ash was of the Satan's Dawgs. The citizenry wasn't constantly warring with itself in a testosterone-driven dance of death. Violence swirled around the motorcycle club much the way pests invade a summer picnic.

Ash wasn't stupid. He knew other parts of the world experienced war and terrible hardships. However, he imagined the citizens in those countries were mostly the same as everyone else. They wanted the fighting to stop so they could live peacefully with those around them.

None of those thoughts would have occurred to Ash had he not been forcibly removed by the FBI agent. Ash's life was better away from the club, even though he'd spent almost all of it on the run.

"Sorry," Finley said with a sigh. "I used to think cops were the good guys."

"What changed?"

"Netflix. I watched that new docuseries. You know the one? It totally messed with my head."

Ash eyed the desk clerk. He'd heard of Netflix, of course, but he'd never seen it. The last thing he wanted to do was talk about a television show. "Why did the cops ask about Hubie?"

"You think he's involved? I hear they found a bloody hammer."

"It wasn't bloody," Ash said.

"How do you know?"

"One of the cops said."

"Still." Finley put his hands on his knees. "I called for Hubie, but he hasn't responded. Isn't that suspicious what with the hammer and all?"

Even though Hubert Dunn was the sole maintenance technician working, it didn't mean he was the only person with access to the basement. All hotel employees went down there to punch their timecards and get a handheld radio.

Any staff member could simply walk over and pick up a tool from the workbench. Ash had used various tools since his time started with the hotel. Occasionally, it was to fix something for a guest. Other times to make a quick repair while the maintenance technicians were engaged in different projects.

Ash tried to remember a time when he used one of the hotel's hammers, but he couldn't pinpoint any. That didn't mean his fingerprints wouldn't be on the tool. He might have moved a hammer to pick up a different implement. Ash couldn't be certain and that worried him.

What if his fingerprints were on the hammer found near Ramon's body? Detective Landry would focus solely on Ash then. It would take some time for the police lab to pull the prints, then run them through the system. Ash didn't want to be around for that. It was bad enough to get arrested and thrown in prison under his real name. At least he'd committed those acts.

He didn't want to get arrested with a new name for a crime he hadn't committed, especially when he was trying to be a better man.

"They asked about Nadine, too," Finley said.

"I know." Ash scanned the lobby.

"I believe you saw her." Finley looked around, too. "Why isn't she here now?"

"That's a good question."

Officer Greenway ended his conversation with the other officers. He looked over his shoulder and noticed Finley. "Hey, you!" he shouted. "Get away from him."

The clerk stood. "I better get back." Under his breath, he said. "Good luck."

Finley returned to the front desk.

***

Ten minutes later, Nadine Delacroix walked through the entrance doors and into the hotel lobby. She wore the same clothes Ash had seen her in earlier. Her slouchy purse remained on her right shoulder, although it seemed considerably lighter now. The manager glanced around, her eyes widening in surprise. She hurried toward the nearest cop, which happened to be Officer Greenway.

While they spoke, Nadine's gaze bounced about the lobby, taking in all the law enforcement activity. Eventually, her eyes landed on Ash, and the two exchanged glances. Unlike before, her stare lingered on him for a couple of seconds. She nodded in response to something Greenway said, and her attention moved toward the north hallway. Greenway pointed in the direction she was looking.

Nadine said, "Oh, no!" and quickly covered her mouth. Her gaze snapped back to Ash. This time, her eyes were hard and judgmental.

The officer put his hand on the manager's shoulder in a comforting way. He said something more, and she nodded once again, pulling her attention away from Ash. The two walked toward the edge of the lobby and disappeared into the north hallway.

Ash stood. He knew the score now.

No local cop would give him a fair shake, especially where a murder was concerned. He couldn't imagine Lester Krumland taking his side in this matter, either. The marshal might have career trouble, so if Ash ended up in a Georgia jail, it might not be the worst thing for Krumland. He could wash his hands of Ash and fix whatever job problem he might have.

If Ash wanted to clear his relatively new name, it was up to him.

He hated to leave the lobby before Travis was found. However, Ash had a bad feeling about how this day would turn out if he didn't do something immediately to help himself. He slowly backed away from the fountain. His head swiveled left and right as he searched for any cop looking in his direction. None did.

Ash turned and bumped into Thelma Bennett. She looked up at him with big eyes and a wavering smile. Her pencil hovered over her notebook. "Where're you going?" she asked.

"Anywhere else." Ash glanced over his shoulder. Still, no cops looked in his direction. He needed to get moving.

Thelma asked, "Don't you have to talk with the police some more?"

"They can wait." He headed toward the south hallway, not bothering to say goodbye to Thelma.

She hurried next to his side. "What're you doing?"

Ash looked down at her, then quickened his pace. "Do me a favor and keep it down."

She struggled to keep up with him, glancing back toward the lobby as they went. "There's been a murder."

"I know."

"A real-life murder." Thelma struggled to catch her breath as they hurried into the south corridor. "Do you know what this means?"

Ash knew exactly what it meant. His friend was dead, the cops suspected his involvement, and his cover would soon be blown. Worse than all that, Travis was missing and he might not get to spend another moment with Daphne Winterbourne. He walked into the elevator lobby and jammed the Up button with his thumb.

"We can solve this," Thelma said, "and clear your name." She anxiously tapped her pencil against her notepad. "That's something Travis McGee and Parker would do."

Ash considered the older woman. Mentioning the names of the protagonists from his favorite books was a nice touch. Thelma was a natural saleswoman. In a similar situation, McGee would certainly work to clear his name like Ash wanted to do now. Parker, on the other hand, would simply walk away and get a new name. The latter was too close to the man Ash had been. McGee was more like the man he wanted to be.

Thelma pointed the eraser end of her pencil at Ash. "Haven't you ever wanted to solve a murder?"

He had solved several crimes since arriving in the Witness Protection Program. Until then, it was a skillset he didn't know he had. Although it wasn't much different from the talents he used as the Satan's Dawgs bookkeeper.

Find a problem. Determine its cause. Stop the problem.

Some of Ash's solutions while with the club were more permanent than others. That was his role and one he did well.

Recently, though, Ash found problems, determined their causes, and turned over what he discovered to the police. The lack of brutal solutions didn't bother him. In fact, he felt better about himself when he didn't need to be violent.

The elevator dinged, announcing its arrival.

"I'll look into it," Ash said.

"What about me?" Thelma's brow furrowed and confusion filled her eyes. "What about the Bookworms?"

The elevator doors opened, and Ash stepped

inside. Thelma followed him.

"The cops think I killed the concierge," he said.

"I know," Thelma said. Her brow furrowed. "You didn't, right?"

"He was my friend."

"See? I knew it. I have a sense for these things. Besides, if you did kill that man, you would have run away just now. Not hung around to talk with me."

She had a point. Ash pressed the button for the third floor and the elevator doors slowly closed.

"What's on three?" Thelma asked.

"A maintenance man."

Her eyes widened. "You think he might be involved?"

Ash didn't think so, but he couldn't be sure. He said, "Only one way to know."

"Ask some questions." Thelma smiled as the elevator moved upward. "I knew I liked you from the moment we met."

Chapter 9

The elevator doors opened, and Ash stepped into the third-floor hallway. He had the option to go left or right which led north and south respectively.

"So," Thelma Bennett said, "who's this fella we're looking for?"

"His name is Hubie."

"What's he doing up here?"

"Fixing a leak."

Thelma cocked her head. "What room?"

"I don't know."

"Then how did you know he was on this floor, then?"

"He told me," Ash said. "Plus, he said it on the radio."

"How long ago was that?"

Ash couldn't say because he didn't wear a watch. "Some time, I guess."

"Which means he could be anywhere by now." Thelma waved her hand, dismissing her own thought. "That's assuming he told the truth in the first place."

"How's that?"

"If he was involved in the concierge's murder, he'd want to throw people off his trail, right? What better way than to say he was working on the third floor instead of going to the stairwell to meet a soon-to-be dead man?"

Ash raised an eyebrow.

"Or not," Thelma said with a shrug. "My imagination gets away from me at times. Maybe this maintenance fella was really fixing something up here."

"I hope so," Ash said.

He moved a couple of steps toward the north corridor. Ash couldn't see all the rooms because of the bending hallway. All the room doors he could see seemed closed since no light poured into the hallway. He hurried south. Even though this corridor had the same bend as the other, he saw a cleaning cart midway down the hallway. Light spilled out of the nearby room and illuminated the floor.

"We don't have much to go on, do we?" Thelma asked. "We're winging it."

"Got a better idea?" Ash started down the south corridor.

"Oh, no," Thelma said, hurrying to catch up. "Lots of amateur detectives wing it. It's sort of their modus operandi. Maybe it's even a trope."

Ash looked over his shoulder. "Trope?"

"A reoccurring theme." Thelma waved her notepad. "Of course, winging it doesn't come without its dangers."

"How so?"

"The police don't like it when amateurs get involved. Boy, you're really moving." She hurried to keep up with his long strides. "Irritable cops might be a trope, too. I wonder if the cops really mind when someone snoops around and solves one of their cases."

Ash knew from experience how the police felt when someone interfered with an investigation. They were never happy to have a do-gooder poking around, even if it resulted in a closed case and a captured suspect. It reflected badly on their promise to serve and protect.

"Then there are the bad guys," Thelma added.

"Bad guys?" Ash slowed his pace as he neared the open room.

"The killers," Thelma said. "In a murder mystery, they always try to stop the hero from solving the crime. Maybe that's a trope, too."

"Makes sense."

"Now that I'm thinking about it," Thelma said as she struggled to catch her breath. "Maybe I don't understand tropes. It seems like the cops and the bad guys both want to stop the protagonist."

"That's how it works in real life," Ash said. He stepped past the cleaning cart and leaned into the empty room. "Hello?"

Emily Larson appeared from around the corner with a pillow clutched in her hands. She looked tired. Being the only working member of the cleaning crew had to be exhausting. Her eyebrows rose in a questioning manner. "Yes?"

"Seen Hubie?"

Emily walked forward, still clutching the pillow in her arms. She smiled awkwardly at Ash, then Thelma. "He's fixing a leak or something."

"Which room?"

The cleaning woman stepped into the hallway and looked to the south. "He was in three-oh-eight. The guest arrives tomorrow. They always reserve the same room whenever they come."

"Thank you," Ash said. He walked away.

Thelma scampered after him. "Shouldn't we have asked her more questions?"

"I got what I needed."

"She looked scared." Thelma glanced back over her shoulder. "Maybe she saw someone or knows something related to the murder."

"She's timid," Ash said, recalling a word he'd recently read in a John D. MacDonald novel. "That's how she is."

"Still, we should have asked a couple more questions." Disappointment filled Thelma's voice. Her pencil hovered over her notepad. There wasn't much written on it.

Ash stopped in front of room 308. Its door remained slightly open. The slightest tug would have secured the lock. Usually, the room doors shut automatically because of the pneumatic hardware attached to them.

"Do the employees have master keys?" Thelma asked.

"Only the cleaning staff and maintenance crew." Ash pushed the door open. He wasn't worried about leaving fingerprints. His prints were all over the hotel. "Hubie?" Ash paused for a second before stepping into the room. Thelma closely followed him, bumping into his back.

The door automatically closed behind them with a metallic latch.

It only took a moment for Ash to check the room. The room was made up and ready for a guest's arrival. An aroma of cleaning products hung in the air.

"No one's here," Thelma said. She glanced around. "What leak was this Hubie guy supposed to be fixing?"

"Don't know." Ash surveyed the room again, then moved to the bathroom. Everything seemed to be in order. "Must not have been hard because he's already done."

"Isn't that weird?"

Ash shrugged. "Hubie's pretty good at his job." He looked under the counter but didn't see anything out of the ordinary. "Might have been an easy fix."

"Not that," Thelma said. She motioned toward the door. "Why leave it open the way it was?"

"Maybe he was coming back."

"He has a key, right? No reason to leave it unsecured that way."

Ash put his hands on his hips. "Maybe he went to get something heavy and didn't want to put it down to open the door."

"If it was that heavy, wouldn't he use a dolly and take the elevator? Then he could use his key without a problem. See what I mean?" Thelma hurriedly jotted something on her notepad. "Or perhaps he unlocked it for someone else."

"Maybe."

"Or." Thelma looked up. "Perhaps that Emily woman left the room unlocked. The room smells freshly cleaned. What if she and Hubie were in the room together?"

"Doing what?"

"I don't know. That's why we should ask more questions."

"Maybe it was just an accident," Ash said, "and the door just didn't close fully."

Thelma pointed at the door. "It latched for us. No problem."

Ash considered the telephone on the nightstand near the bed. In a situation like this, he should call the marshal's hot line again. Ash's current identity would surely be exposed as a fraud once the police really dug into it. However, if he got hold of someone and told them the situation, they'd insist he leave Coastal Haven immediately.

However, he didn't want to go yet. Ash wanted to see Daphne Winterbourne once more. He needed to find Travis. Plus, he hoped to clear his name, even if it was assumed.

Ash was accused of many crimes while he was a Dawg. Most of which he did. Since he entered the Witness Protection Program, he strove to be a better man. Being accused of a crime now bothered Ash, even if he could simply walk away and start a new life under a different name. That might not be as easy as previous incidents due to Lester Krumland.

"We should go back and interview the cleaning lady," Thelma said, "while we have the chance." She headed toward the door. "You coming?"

Ash pulled his gaze from the phone on the nightstand. "Yeah."

Thelma yanked open the door and stepped into the hallway. "Well, would you look at that? She's gone."

The cleaning cart was no longer there.

"I bet we spooked her," Thelma said, "and she took off."

"She's doing the work of the entire crew today."

Thelma tapped the pencil eraser against her teeth. "You think the cleaning crews work from the upper floors to the lower? Or vice versa?"

"Even if we knew, the entire system went out the window when most of the staff called in sick."

Ash headed toward the elevators, and Thelma hurried after him. The door to room 308 locked behind them.

"Are we going after the cleaning lady?" she asked.

He didn't respond. His mind was ablaze with options. Ash turned into the elevator lobby and pressed the Down button. As an afterthought, he pressed the Up button, too.

"What's the plan?" Thelma asked.

"We split up."

Thelma scratched her head with the tip of her pencil. "You're not trying to ditch me, are you? Because I can get the rest of the Bookworms up here and we could help search for the cleaning lady."

"Wouldn't look good," Ash said. "Me with a

bunch of ladies will attract attention.”

“Right. Right.” Thelma tapped her front teeth with the pencil eraser. “Gotta keep a low profile and all that jazz. Smart.”

The first elevator dinged, and the Up arrow illuminated. The doors slowly opened.

“Although,” Thelma said, “if we’re hunting a killer, maybe I shouldn’t go alone. You seem much more capable of handling that kind of situation than I.”

It was a good argument. Ash remembered some of the TV shows his grandmother watched. He often wondered how the amateur sleuth escaped harm while hunting down a variety of killers. In the books Ash enjoyed, Travis McGee was a tall man with wartime experience while Parker was a career criminal with a cruel demeanor. They could handle themselves in a pinch.

The entertaining ladies with their charming dispositions in his grandmother’s shows seemed ripe for trouble to befall them. Ash didn’t want to put Thelma in any type of danger.

“We should call it off,” he said. It was a hollow suggestion since he only wanted her to stop. He had no intention of stopping.

“Call it off? No way. Look at what we found.” She pointed in the direction of room 308. “That room was left open for a reason. The police don’t know that. Only we do.”

The elevator doors closed. When they did, the Down arrow lit up, and the doors reopened.

Thelma hurried inside. “Are you coming?”

He grunted softly, then entered the elevator.

"Where to?" Thelma asked.

"The basement."

"Oh, I like the sound of that." She pressed the button labeled B, and the elevator started its descent. "All sorts of crimes happen in basements."

When the elevator doors opened, Ash leaned out and glanced in both directions. He was concerned a police officer might be in the basement looking for Hubie. Heck, they might be looking for him, too. It had been more than a few minutes since Ash walked away from the main lobby.

No one appeared to be down there, though. Ash checked left and right once more.

"This might be too personal," Thelma said, "but are you married?"

Ash held up a hand for her to be quiet.

"I told you about my daughter, right?" Thelma whispered. "Whip smart and beautiful, like I was growing up."

Nearby, the hotel's heating system droned on. Ash strained to hear anyone or anything above the noise. He stepped out, tentatively, but still didn't see anyone.

"She'll be here soon," Thelma said. "She couldn't get away from her work any earlier."

Ash headed toward the maintenance area. Thelma tagged along.

"Kinsey," Thelma said, her voice rising with excitement. "That's her name. Named after Sue Grafton's detective, of course."

Ash was momentarily distracted by that. He'd read one of Grafton's books and remembered her detective, Kinsey Millhone. Being around the group of mystery readers let him feel like a member of a new club.

Thelma continued. "She moved to Florida after college to work for a TV station. I can't wait for you to meet her. You're gonna love her. Maybe you two could get a coffee or something."

Ash said, "There's a woman."

"Oh," Thelma said, disappointment registering in her eyes. "Is it serious?"

"I'd like it to be."

"It's not official, then?" Hope filled Thelma's voice. "Perhaps you need to keep your options open."

Ash didn't want to get into a relationship discussion right then, especially one that could never occur for a variety of reasons. He refocused his attention on the task at hand. Everything in the maintenance area appeared as it had been when he'd been down there earlier with Hubie. Nothing was disturbed on the workbenches. Yet someone had been in the basement while Ash had talked with Officer Greenway near Ramon's body.

"Kinsey loves this conference," Thelma said. "She started covering the weekend anchor position last year, so she was afraid she might miss the event. She's a smart one, I tell you. She convinced her station to let her do a story about it.”

Ash glanced at the rollaway bed set up in the corner, his home for the next few days. The corner of the wool blanket was flipped up, exposing what was underneath. His small travel bag was there, as was a small cardboard box. Nearby was the cat’s litter box.

“Hey,” Thelma said. “Is this where you’re sleeping? Seems like a health code violation. A safety violation, if not. How do you sleep down here with all the noise?”

Ash squatted next to the bed. He positioned his hands at the corners of the box, hoping to lessen any chance of getting his fingerprints on it. Clear packing tape covered most of it.

“What’s that?” Thelma asked, moving closer.

“The manuscript.”

“The missing one?” She bent at her hips to get a better view of the box. “Are you serious?”

He nodded.

“That’s why the concierge was murdered.” Thelma straightened as she waggled her finger at the box. “Whoever took it put it under there, so you’d get blamed for it.”

“That’s what I’m thinking.”

Thelma tapped his shoulder. “We’re good at this, huh? I wish the rest of the girls were here for this. They’d get a kick out of it.”

Ash moved the box left and right, still careful not to get any prints on its surface.

“Clever,” she said.

He looked up at her with a quizzical look on

his face.

"Checking to see if it's open, right? Once we know who wrote the manuscript, we can look for any collectors attending the conference."

Except that wasn't what Ash was doing. Since the box remained closed, Ash hoped to find some evidence that might lead to a killer. A bloody fingerprint, perhaps. Maybe some substance that would give a clear direction— smeared make-up, a splat of ketchup, or a glob of mechanic's grease. However, no foreign materials were on the box.

"A collector might have motive to steal the manuscript," Thelma said, "but what's the motivation to kill the concierge? To get it for free? I guess that would work. Greed is always an incentive for murder."

Ash's expression tightened as he considered why someone pushed the manuscript under the rollaway bed.

Thelma cleared her throat. "I hate to ask, but you do have a place of your own, right?"

He looked up at her. "Excuse me?"

"I mean, you're not really sleeping down here because this is your home?" She patted the edge of the rollaway.

"I've got an apartment," he muttered and turned his attention back to the box.

"The flood was real?"

Ash lifted the box by its corners and looked underneath it. No clues were there, either.

"I'm only asking," Thelma said, "because my daughter has moved beyond her phase of rescuing men. Not that you need rescuing or anything." She glanced around. "I'm just saying you should have seen the fellas Kinsey brought home during that time. Sheesh." Thelma's eyes widened. "Although, I shouldn't say it like that. It's not like she has a revolving door in the relationship department."

Ash dropped the box to the floor, then stood.

"Kinsey's man-picker was broken is what I'm trying to say." Thelma chuckled to herself. "Although I probably shouldn't even be saying that much."

Ash put his boot against the box and pushed it back to where he had found it.

"What're you doing?" Thelma cocked her head. "Shouldn't we alert the police and tell them what we found?"

"And say what? That the missing manuscript is under my bed?"

"I was with you when you found it. I'll be your alibi."

Ash shook his head. "That's not how they'll look at it."

Thelma searched his eyes before a realization set in. "Oh. They'll say you put it there to throw them off the trail."

"Or they'll say I was stupid."

"You wouldn't put it there, though. You're too smart to do that." Thelma's eyes widened. "Not that you're a killer. You're too nice for that." As if to prove it to herself, she motioned at the litter box. "You have a kitty, too. Killers don't have cats."

Ash was pretty sure that wasn't true, but it was nice to know at least one person here believed in his innocence, even if it was due to Travis. "Whoever left the manuscript here might come back for it."

"It doesn't make sense to do that." Thelma shook her head. "If the concierge had the manuscript and someone killed him for it, they wouldn't leave it behind unless…" Her thought trailed off.

"They didn't know it was valuable."

"Why take it at all then?" Thelma's gaze drifted to the ceiling. "Unless the killer took it to point the blame at you. We're right back where we started."

It was a possibility. Ash thought about Knuckles, the tough guy looking for Ramon. However, Ash didn't want to get tunnel vision on the man. He'd been in situations like this before and learned not to jump to conclusions.

"Or maybe," Thelma continued, "the manuscript's theft and the concierge's murder are not connected at all." She held up two fingers. "If that's the case, we should be investigating two crimes, not one. A killer *and* a thief."

"It's possible," Ash said.

He considered Thelma's suggestion and thought about Nadine's heavy purse. If she indeed took the manuscript, the concierge was alive when she left the storage room. Ash had seen Ramon stick his head out.

When Nadine returned to the lobby, she did

so through the front doors, acting as if she'd just arrived at the hotel. She seemed surprised by the news of Ramon's murder. If she had taken the manuscript, she could have walked it out to her car. Unless she never took the manuscript in the first place. If that was the case, why did her purse appear heavier after she visited with Ramon? Also, where had she gone after leaving him?

Ash needed to consider other suspects and not get focused solely on the hotel manager either. Perhaps someone else stole the manuscript, but feared they were about to be discovered with it. They hid it underneath Ash's bed to avoid detection. When Ramon was subsequently murdered, it stopped the thief from returning to the basement. Perhaps the bandit would come back later and retrieve it. Maybe they wrote off the theft as a loss and would never return. The variables were too many to waste much time thinking about them.

Thelma tapped her pencil against the notepad. "Tomorrow night's mystery game is never as complicated as this, since we've only got a couple of hours to play." She looked at him conspiratorially. "You know, the authors never play with us. I think they're too afraid of not looking as sharp as some of their characters."

Ash pulled the corner of the blanket down, obscuring the box hidden under the bed.

"What's the next step?" Thelma asked.

"We get out of here."

"We're not going to catch a thief?" She pointed

at a darkened corner. "We could wait over there until the bad guy shows back up, then spring on him like a cat." She lifted her left hand in the air, fingers spread apart. "Rawr."

Ash couldn't tell her about his background. He also couldn't share his worries about the local cops peeling apart his fabricated history until they discovered the truth. It had happened before with a capable investigator. He suspected the Marlowe Bay police would be diligent and resourceful in their search.

"Do you have a cell phone?" Ash asked.

Thelma nodded but a frown formed. "It's up in my room. I don't carry it around once I get to the conference."

Ash stepped over to the docking stations and pulled out a fully charged radio.

"Need to call someone?" Thelma asked.

"Not yet."

"Can I have one?" she motioned to the radio. "In case we get separated."

Ash shrugged. He didn't want a partner, but Thelma was on his side and may be helpful, especially since he would have trouble moving around the hotel. The cops were probably searching for him now.

He pulled a radio from the docking station and set it on channel 4, a frequency used for private conversations. The rest of the hotel staff used the first three channels, depending on their job responsibilities. "You can call me on this if we get separated."

Thelma smiled as she took the radio. "What

names should we use?"

Ash pointed at his nametag.

"No, no. Like shouldn't we have callsigns like Maverick and Goose?"

He understood the *Top Gun* reference, even if he never made it through the movie. Some of the other Dawgs had watched it one night. Ash couldn't remember why he hadn't finished it but was certain it was for club business.

"Ash is fine," he said.

"That's no fun." Thelma waggled the radio. "How about this? I'll be Miss Marple and you be Hercule Poirot." Her smile broadened.

"Who?"

"Agatha Christie's famous detective. You should try her books since you love reading the oldies."

He shrugged. "Call me whatever you like." Ash headed for the southern stairwell.

Thelma scampered after him. When she caught up, she asked, "Where are we going?"

"To get some answers."

Chapter 10

Ash ascended the concrete stairs quietly, constantly leaning over the railing to look toward the upper levels. With each careful step, his body remained coiled, ready to spring in whatever direction was necessary.

The silence in the stairwell was not experienced anywhere else in the building. The heating system's hum, which had been a constant drone in the basement, was absent here. It was so silent that even a scrape of a shoe sole across a concrete step reverberated up and down the stairwell.

"What's your kitty's name?" Thelma asked with a slight wheeze. It wasn't a long climb, only a single floor.

"Travis," he whispered.

"Like McGee?"

He nodded. Ash named his cat after John D. MacDonald's famous amateur sleuth. The tom had lived in the bookstore Ash ran while in Pleasant Valley, Maine. That was his first placement in the Witness Protection Program. Travis's former owner insisted customers call the cat whatever they pleased. Supposedly, she thought felines reflected the personality of whoever they were with at the time. The only rule to her naming convention was the choice needed to be based upon a mystery character.

He didn't explain any of that to Thelma, though. There wasn't time since they reached the first-floor landing. Ash pulled open the door, just enough to peek through. Dozens of people milled aimlessly about the conference hall. Almost all appeared happy, and many carried at least one book.

Thelma stood behind the partially opened door. She put her hands on her hips and exhaled heavily. "Not used to walking stairs anymore. Guess I'm out of shape."

For a couple of seconds, Ash held the door open just a crack, watching the activity in the hall.

"Kinsey," Thelma said, "that's my daughter, in case you forgot."

Ash hadn't.

"She walks the stairs all the time. Keeps her in tip-top shape. Gotta be that way for sharing the local news on TV. You know what they say about the camera adding ten pounds and all."

"No cops," Ash said and closed the door.

Thelma's eyebrows lifted. "That's good. Right?"

Ash pulled the portable radio from his belt and turned it on. He ensured the scan function was still selected so he could hear all channels. Almost immediately, the device beeped, signaling a channel switch. Its display screen illuminated with a bright orange.

Nadine Delacroix broadcasted on the hotel's primary channel. "*All cleaning staff, porters, and maintenance personnel to the lobby."*

Since only Emily, Hubie, and Ash were working due to the outbreak, it seemed an odd request. Why not address them by names? Perhaps she didn't know the extent of absentees. That was unlikely. Even though she'd been sick, surely Finley or Ramon would have kept her apprised. Maybe it was an act for the cops. In order to show them she wasn't up to speed on the day's events. If that was the reason, why would she need the police to believe she hadn't been informed?

Ash turned down the radio's volume and clipped it to his belt. "Here's the deal," he said. Ash tapped lightly on the closed door. "There are a lot of people out there."

"Probably waiting for the opening ceremonies." Thelma nodded. "That's what I'd be doing if we weren't working this case."

Ash furrowed his brow. "When we step through this door, we need to blend in, so no one pays any attention to us."

"It's a mystery conference. There are some really famous people here." She smiled almost apologetically. "No one will even notice us. Trust me."

"I'm sure the cops are looking for me now," Ash said. "Maybe someone out there knows that."

"My dear." Thelma patted his arm in the comforting way his grandmother used to do. "You're overthinking this. No one is going to pay any attention to you, let alone me."

"Let's hope that's true."

Ash pulled open the door, and the two stepped into the conference lobby.

Immediately, a woman hollered from across the room, "Thelma!" A dark-haired woman in a black sweatshirt waved her hand high in the air. For a moment, she looked questioningly at Ash, then turned her attention back to his companion. "Thelma!" the woman shouted again. "Over here."

All the heads in the immediate vicinity spun toward the waving attendee, then they turned in Ash's direction, looking for the object of the shouting woman's excitement.

Thelma cringed. "Sorry." She lifted her hand and tentatively waved back. "She's with the Bookworms."

The dark-haired woman hurried across the conference hall. Other attendees watched her weave in and out of the crowd.

Ash sidestepped along the back wall. "I've gotta go."

"What about the mystery?" Thelma asked. "We haven't solved it yet."

"I can't do it with a crowd."

"The Bookworms can help."

Ash didn't stop shuffling sideways.

"I understand," Thelma said with a reluctant nod. She waggled her handheld radio. "We'll call if we find anything."

Ash turned and hurried away.

"Keep notes!" Thelma called out.

Ash politely nodded at several conference attendees as he hurried along the nearby wall. He felt like a mouse scurrying away from trouble. More accurately, he'd say he felt like a rat scuttling along the wall, since turning on the Satan's Dawgs is what landed him in this trouble.

The gathered attendees barely registered his existence now that he was away from Thelma. It was a truth associated with his job: most guests ignored the hotel staff. He'd experienced that same indifference while working as an amusement park custodian in Lindo Gato, Texas. The lack of consideration suited Ash fine.

The hallway wound around a cluster of meeting rooms and led back to the main corridor. Up ahead, the crowd flowed around two people. Conference president Sylvia Grayson spoke with Detective Landry. The investigator nodded as he wrote in his notepad. She waved her arms as she spoke, a flightless bird trying to escape gravity's pull.

Landry lifted his head and started to look in Ash's direction.

He stepped into the nearest room to avoid discovery. Rows of chairs faced a raised dais. A table sat on the stage with a black cloth draped over it. Four microphones waited silently in front of the same number of seats. On the farthest wall was a door that led to the staff hallway.

"Look," a woman said from Ash's right. "It's him."

He tensed as he turned.

A group of seven women in yellow T-shirts clustered together. Each Mystery Maven held a pen and notepad. They eyed Ash with varying levels of suspicion.

"The porter," Estelle Enderby muttered.

Maxine Coleman pointed. "The cops are looking for him."

"I didn't do it." Ash raised his hands in surrender.

"Didn't steal the manuscript," Estelle said, "or didn't kill the concierge?"

"Either."

"What else *would* he say?" a woman in the back of the group asked. "It's not like he'd admit to murdering that fella."

"He could admit to theft," a second suggested, "if he was a stand-up guy."

"What if he's telling the truth?" a woman with pink hair asked. "Like it's a case of mistaken identity or something."

"Maybe," Maxine said with obvious excitement, "he's being framed."

"Oh, brother." Estelle rolled her eyes. "Gimme a break."

Ash briefly thought about telling them about the manuscript tucked under his rollaway bed but quickly realized introducing that information into this group might be hazardous to his freedom.

"I'm serious." Maxine glanced at her friends.

"Perhaps the cops are focused on the wrong suspect."

"That happens all the time in the books," the woman with pink hair said. "The movies, too."

Ash moved away from the room's opening. He didn't want Detective Landry or Sylvia Grayson to walk by and spot him. "Ramon was my friend," he whispered. "I wouldn't hurt him."

Several of the ladies looked among themselves, apparently wondering if they should believe his denial.

"Besides," Ash said quickly, "why would I take the manuscript? I don't know anything about it."

"You knew it was valuable," Estelle said. "What more do we need to know?"

Ash shrugged a single shoulder. "Ramon knew it was valuable, so did Sylvia."

"Ah-hah!" the woman with pink hair said, her demeanor suddenly changing. "Maybe he did do it."

"Pipe down, Phyllis," Estelle said. "We haven't forgotten about you not registering Maxie's and my rooms."

Phyllis looked at her notepad and muttered, "It was an accident."

"If I did steal it," Ash said, "who would I sell it to?"

"That's a good point." Maxine nodded. "Do we even know anything about the manuscript?"

The Mystery Mavens exchanged glances.

"It was supposed to be a surprise," Estelle said. "Some big reveal to get the auction bidding wound up."

"Maybe it's a red herring," Phyllis said softly, still not looking up from her notepad.

Estelle scoffed. "It's not a red herring."

"Then a MacGuffin." Phyllis looked up now, glancing at her friends for an affirmative response. "You know, like the statue in *The Maltese Falcon*."

"It's not a MacGuffin, either." Estelle tsked. "That doesn't happen in real life. Get a clue."

Phyllis lowered her head again. "They could happen," she said under her breath. "Real life or not."

"Well," Maxine said, "I vote he's being framed."

Estelle waved off her friend. "We're not taking a poll, Maxie." She faced Ash. "What can you tell us about the concierge? Did he have any enemies? Did he owe anyone money?"

Ash's gaze drifted over the various faces of the assembled women.

"You can trust us," Maxine said. Several of the woman nodded behind her. "If you're innocent, we can help prove it."

"What if he's not?" Estelle asked. "We can't start believing him for no reason."

"He's not going to tell us anything if we don't give him the benefit of the doubt."

Phyllis added, "Maybe he knows something, but he doesn't know he knows it."

Estelle's face pinched. "Don't strain yourself, Phyllis."

"Listen," Maxine said, "we've read mysteries

for years.”

“Decades,” one of the Mavens added.

“Watched them on TV, too,” another said.

Maxine continued. “We know a lot about solving crimes. If you trust us, we can help you.”

Ash considered all the Mavens once more before saying, “I’m looking for a guy in a leather jacket and a white hooded sweatshirt.”

“Why?” Maxine asked. “Is he the killer?”

The other Mystery Mavens leaned in, anxiously waiting for Ash’s reply. Phyllis hurriedly scribbled in her notebook.

Ash said, “He was asking about Ramon.”

“Before the murder?” Estelle asked.

“Maybe they were friends,” Maxine suggested.

“They weren’t,” Ash said. “He worked for Ramon’s bookie, some guy named Mr. Leo. It sounded like Ramon owed money, and the guy in the leather jacket was here to collect.”

“Ah-hah!” Phyllis said. “The bookie killed Ramon.”

Estelle scoffed. “What’d I say about popping off, Phyllis? If the bookie killed Ramon, how would he get paid back? Huh?”

Phyllis tightened her lips. “Maybe Ramon paid off his debt with the manuscript, but the thug killed him to make it look like he hadn’t. That’s what happened in one of Mason Freemantle’s stories.”

“*The Louisville Parlay*?” Estelle scoffed. “That was a terrible book.”

“So?” Phyllis said. “Doesn’t make it untrue.”

“That’s exactly what it means. You

Freemantles—" Estelle finished her thought with a smirk and a shake of her head.

Phyllis waved her hand. "What I'm saying is this: the concierge stole the manuscript, gave it to the bookie's collector, and was killed in return to make it looked like he hadn't paid." A prideful smile formed on Phyllis's lips. "Mason Freemantle had it right all along."

Maxine crossed her arms. "Although the protagonist in that book wasn't a concierge, was he?"

"He was a waiter," Phyllis said. "Big deal. Same difference."

"If I remember correctly…" Maxine looked at the ceiling. "It wasn't a manuscript either. It was a winning lottery ticket the waiter wanted to trade."

Phyllis clucked. "You're splitting hairs. The waiter had a winning slip from the horse races. Other than that, this is the same situation as *The Louisville Parlay*."

"No," Maxine said. "It's not. A betting slip can be redeemed by the holder. How does someone go about selling a manuscript without calling attention to themselves?"

"I'm with Maxie," Estelle said. "If the concierge stole the manuscript to cover his debt, the bookie's thug would have made him sell it. Cash is king, as they say."

The other Mystery Mavens murmured their support.

Estelle continued. "In this case, the concierge would be forced to take the risk of finding a buyer and maybe getting caught by the cops. That way the bookie could continue to add interest—"

"The vigorish," Maxine interrupted.

"—until the concierge brought his account current. A bank never cuts off a client they believe will make good on a loan."

Estelle made a good argument, but Ash knew that's not how it worked. He'd known several bookies who put late-payers in the ground. It was a cost of doing business and a simple way to send a message to future bettors to bring their accounts current in a timely fashion.

Maxine faced Ash. "We'll help you find this guy in a leather jacket, but we want to be there when you talk with him." Before Ash could ask why, she added, "We're in a race with the Beautiful Bookworms to solve this murder first." She grinned at her friends. "Tomorrow's mystery dinner will be a cinch after this."

Phyllis sighed. "We won't get a trophy for solving this murder, though."

Estelle rolled her eyes. "We'll get bragging rights. Solving a real-life homicide is worth way more than some plastic trophy."

"We should ask Vivienne Hart to help," Maxine said.

Several of the Mavens smiled and nodded at the idea.

Estelle sighed. "The authors never help. Plus, if she did, the Bookworms could hold it over our heads. Win or lose, it's no good for us."

There seemed no way for Ash to escape this

moment. If he turned and ran, the Mavens would turn him into the police. Better to have them on his side than working against him. Ash took the radio from his belt. He stopped the scan function and set the channel to 5, another frequency for private conversations. Ash handed the device to Estelle. "Call me on this."

"You don't have one now," Maxine said. "It takes two for a conversation."

"I'll get another one. Also, keep an eye out for my cat."

Several of the ladies oohed at the mention of the tom.

Ash added, "He's running loose through the hotel now."

"Oh, a cat." A Maven in the back clapped her hands. "Now, this mystery is *purr*-fect."

"No, it's not," another disagreed, "A missing kitty is a cat-astrophe."

A third pointed toward the exit. "We don't have time to waste. Let's find that cat, right meow."

Estelle shushed them. "Knock that off. This is serious." She turned back to Ash. "You told the policeman you brought your cat to work today."

"My apartment was flooded."

"You should never bring a cat into an environment like this," Estelle said. "It could traumatize the poor baby."

Maxine nodded in agreement. "Kitties need a calm, peaceful environment."

"Maybe it's a mouser," Phyllis said. "You never know, it could have fun being here."

Estelle curled her lip. "You're a dog person, Phyllis. Stay in your lane."

"What's your kitty's name?" Maxine asked.

"Travis," Ash said. "Named after Travis McGee, of course."

Maxine crinkled her nose. "Travis?"

"It's a perfectly good name," Ash said defensively.

The gathered women didn't seem to agree.

"It's paw-ful," one of the women said.

"A naming faux-paw," another added, miming a cat scratching.

"All right," Estelle snapped at her friends. "That's enough."

Ash was thankful he hadn't shared the naming rule with them.

"We're wasting time," Estelle said, waving the portable radio. "We've got a bookie's enforcer to find."

"Don't forget a kitty," Maxine added.

The Mavens left the room together, a school of yellow fish searching for a shark.

And a cat.

Chapter 11

Ash didn't return to the main corridor like the Mystery Mavens. Instead, he hurried across the meeting room, opened the door, and stepped into a brightly lit hallway. This corridor ran the length of the conference center, allowing servers to deliver meals, snacks, and coffee to the various meeting rooms. He turned left and headed toward the kitchen, which was at the far end.

Usually, the noise from meal prep drifted down the narrow corridor. Today, it was unusually quiet. Gone were the loud voices, the clanging of utensils, and the sizzle of a grill.

The only one in the kitchen was the chef, Isaiah Grant. He was a tall, black man with a protruding belly. His white uniform fit him snuggly, and his white cap sat at a jaunty angle. He held a phone to his ear with one hand. The other waved at Ash.

A credit card lay on the cutting board in front of the chef. The door to the loading dock was behind him.

If Ash wanted, he could leave the hotel by bursting through one of its many back doors and make a run for it along the boardwalk. He didn't give it much thought, though. He wanted to clear his name, find Ramon's murderer, and see Daphne Winterbourne once more. Running wasn't an option—at least, not right now.

"That's right," Isaiah said. "Fifty pizzas." His expression soured. "No, this isn't a joke. Our staff is out sick, and we've got an opening ceremony set to start any moment. We need help."

Ash walked through the kitchen and noticed a portable radio sitting on a counter. He glanced at the chef and saw another radio clipped to a pant pocket. "Mind if I take this?"

Isaiah covered the phone's receiver with his free hand. "Go ahead. I sent home the last server after he started coughing."

Ash considered the device. He wasn't typically worried about germs, but this outbreak of the flu gave him pause. He walked over to a sanitizer dispenser and squirted a glob of gel into his palm. He rubbed it between his hands, then slathered the radio with it.

"Add some hot wings," Isaiah said into the phone. "Fifty orders." He sighed. "Yeah, I'm serious. It's your lucky day." He covered the receiver once more. "That mystery president lady was asking about you."

"She ask anything specific?" Ash said.

"Just wanted to know if I saw you." Isaiah dropped his hand from the phone. "Don't forget the breadsticks. We'll take fifty of those, too. What's the total? That's fine, that's fine." He picked up the credit card from the cutting board and read its number.

Ash opened the door nearest him and peeked

into the hallway. He didn't see any cops or the conference president.

Isaiah ended the phone call. "I went to culinary school for this?" He tossed the phone onto the cutting board, then removed his wallet.

"Mind if I use that?" Ash motioned toward the phone.

"Don't you have one?" Isaiah tucked the credit card into the billfold.

"I do, but I can't get to it right now." He shrugged a single shoulder. "The cops took it."

The chef stiffened. "What did they do that for?"

"They think I killed Ramon."

Isaiah rested his hands on the counter and leaned forward. His eyes narrowed as he studied Ash. "Did you?"

"Not a chance. I liked him."

The chef slid the phone toward Ash. "Make it quick and don't leave with it. I'm waiting for a call from one of those temporary staffing companies."

Ash grabbed the phone. He started to dial but paused and looked up. "You haven't seen a cat by chance?"

The chef's face tightened. "What kind of operation do you think we're running here?"

"Never mind," Ash said.

"Seriously, man. We have a good reputation. No cats are allowed in the kitchen."

Ash raised an apologetic hand.

"Think before you ask." Isaiah's tone was exasperated.

He nodded, then turned his attention to the phone. The call was answered on the first ring.

"Big Dog Plumbing." It was the same woman's voice from before. "We're off the leash and ready to bite into your clog."

Hearing her again, he was fully convinced it was a computer.

"I need to schedule some service," Ash said.

"Hello, Mr. Reed. We are here to help. This call is being recorded for quality assurance." A keyboard clacked in the background of the call.

Isaiah crossed his arms as he continued to watch Ash.

"Do you have an emergency situation?" the operator asked.

"Yes."

There was more keyboard clacking now. It sounded the same as the previous noise. "Are you in immediate danger?"

"Sort of."

"I did not understand that response," the monotone woman said. "Please say yes or no."

"Yes," Ash said emphatically. "Can I speak with—"

"Hang up now," the computer interrupted, "and contact the local authorities. Call us back to schedule service after the immediate danger has been resolved."

The call ended.

"Hello?" Ash said. He lowered the phone from his ear. "Shoot."

"Problem?" Isaiah asked.

"Dropped call," he lied. "Need to try again. Is

that cool?"

The chef shrugged with his arms still crossed. "Not like I'm in the middle of anything."

Ash redialed the number.

"Big Dog Plumbing. We're off the leash and ready—"

"I need to schedule some service," Ash blurted.

A keyboard clicked on the other end of the line. "Hello, Mr. Reed," the computer operator said. "We are—"

"Operator."

"—here to help."

"*Operator!*"

"This call is being recorded for—"

"Manager," Ash said loudly. "Get me a manager."

Isaiah stiffened. His lips pressed together, and he slowly shook his head. Obviously, he felt Ash's pain.

The other end of the line went silent except for two bursts of keyboard clacking. Ash imagined the robotic woman was taking time to consider his request.

"Do you wish to speak with a supervisor?" the monotone voice asked.

"Yes," Ash said. "Thank you." He felt stupid for thanking a machine.

Another pause occurred, along with two more surges of keyboard clicking. Perhaps lines of code swirled by on some monitored screen, alerting its viewer there might be a problem.

"Are you in immediate danger?" the operator

asked.

Ash sighed. "Yes."

"Hang up now—"

"I mean no," he said.

"—and contact the local authorities."

"No, no, *no!*"

"Call us back to schedule service after the immediate danger has been resolved."

"Manager," Ash hollered. "Supervisor!"

It was no use. The call discounted.

"Seems like you're having some trouble," Isaiah said with an amused smile.

Ash stabbed the redial button with his finger. "One more time."

"Not slowing me down. I'm waiting for pizzas to be delivered, just like I always imagined doing when they made me chef."

"Bulldog Plumbing," the computer said into Ash's ear. "We're off the leash—"

"Supervisor," he said.

The bursts of keyboard clacking returned. "Do you wish to speak to a supervisor?"

"Yes."

"Are you in immediate danger?"

"Supervisor."

"Yes, sir. Please stand by for the first available supervisor."

A song started, and Ash pulled the phone from his ear.

Isaiah raised an eyebrow. "What now?"

"They put me on hold."

"What kind of outfit are you calling?"

"I'm starting to wonder."

Ash lifted the phone to his ear again. The poppy song continued to play. Its singer stuttered something about a karmic chameleon.

The tune abruptly ended. "All of our supervisors are busy," the operator said. "Would you like to continue to hold or leave a callback number?"

"I'll hold," he interrupted.

"If you choose to leave a callback number," the operator continued, "your place in line will be saved."

Ash repeated, "I'll hold."

"Your wait time is approximately eight minutes."

The song returned, and Ash hung up. He set the phone on the counter and slid it back to the chef.

"Didn't go your way, huh?" Isaiah asked.

Ash shrugged. "Computers."

"Better get used to it. They rule the world. We just haven't accepted it yet."

He waved his appreciation, then left the kitchen by stepping back into the hallway.

***

Ash hurried north toward the elevator lobby. He pushed open a door and peeked out. No one was there. He passed the elevators and peered around the corner.

To the left was the conference hall. Sylvia Grayson and Detective Landry were no longer there. Only a bunch of folks Ash suspected were mystery fans. They smiled and laughed while they talked.

Ash swept his attention to the hotel lobby. A multitude of cops hurried about, clearly excited about something. Detective Landry wasn't in the mix, though. Neither was Officer Greenway, the first cop to arrive.

However, Carrie Fenton and Daphne Winterbourne were there. The two huddled together and watched the police activity with great concern.

Ash stared at Daphne. He remembered their brief time together. The meals, the walks, and their conversations. Even more importantly, he recalled each of their kisses.

If he could, he'd walk to her right now and reveal how he felt since their meeting. He wanted to be a better man for a variety of reasons. Daphne Winterbourne might have been the most important.

Yet he needed to stay away. Her safety was paramount. If any of those hunting him discovered how he felt about her, she'd be in extreme danger. One of the Satan's Dawgs had discovered this, forcing Ash to deal with it in a permanent manner.

He pulled back into the elevator lobby and turned on the portable radio he took from Isaiah, the chef. Ash set it to scan. The radio beeped and switched to channel 4. Its screen illuminated a bright orange.

"*Hercule*," Thelma Bennett said. "*This is Miss Marple*." She sounded out of breath.

Ash lifted the radio and pressed the transmit button. "This is Hercule. Go ahead." He didn't feel foolish for using the code name. While on jobs with the Dawgs, they often used monikers to protect their identities in case the authorities were eavesdropping. It was certainly the first time he hid behind an Agatha Christie character, though.

"*Where are you?*" Thelma asked. "*Wait. Don't tell me.*" She inhaled audibly. "*There are ears everywhere.*"

"What's going on?"

Ash stared at his radio for several moments, waiting for Thelma to respond. He then leaned around the corner to see if anyone was headed his way. In the main lobby, the police scurried about, many rushing toward the north hallway. Thankfully, none moved toward the elevator bank.

Daphne and Carrie were gone, and Ash felt a pang of regret.

He glanced in the opposite direction. A group of silver-haired women in black sweatshirts rushed his way. The Beautiful Bookworms were on the move. A cluster of other attendees hurried behind them in their wake. It seemed as if all were thrilled about something, just like the cops were.

Ash pulled all the way back and stood near the service lobby entrance. He previously didn't want to involve Thelma in this mess. However, he was curious about the Bookworms' urgency and destination.

He lifted the radio to his lips. "Miss Marple," he said. "What's going on?"

Thelma said breathlessly. "*The police found the manuscript.*"

Ash's shoulders slumped. "Where did they find it?"

"*Where we did.*"

Under my rollaway bed, Ash thought. If Detective Landry had any doubt about Ash's involvement in the manuscript's theft and Ramon's subsequent murder, it was likely gone now.

The cluster of mystery fans speedwalked by the elevator bank with Thelma in the lead. She lifted the radio and Ash heard, "*We're headed to the lobby to learn more.*"

One of the Bookworms glanced in his direction as she passed. Ash made eye contact with her, but she didn't slow. A second dragged by before a woman shouted from around the corner, "I saw him!"

Ash grabbed the service entry door and disappeared into the hallway.

***

Ash jogged through the service corridor. As he passed the kitchen, he noticed it was silent. Isaiah Grant, the chef, was gone. He continued down the hallway.

He could pop into any of the meeting rooms or continue the length of the hallway to arrive at the great room where he'd seen a mass of conference attendees earlier. He wanted to talk with many people now. Knuckles, Sylvia, Nadine, and Hubie were at the top of his list.

Ash stopped at the first assembly room he came upon. He opened the door and peaked in. A group of conference attendees stood around chatting. If he walked into this room, all those folks would see him. Ash quietly closed the door and continued down the hall, hoping to find an empty one.

His thoughts returned to Ramon's murder and the missing manuscript.

Knuckles seemed the most likely suspect in the concierge's killing. Ash knew bookies who made examples of late payers. It was a drastic resolution for a bookmaker to take. Ramon hadn't acted like his life was in danger when he spoke with Ash, just that he was in debt and couldn't make good. In a situation like that, Knuckles could have inflicted pain to persuade the concierge to find some money. Broken appendages have a way of inspiring a man to discover a new source of funds.

Talking with the enforcer would answer the question of his involvement once and for all.

Ash stopped at the next meeting room, opened the door, and peered in. Another group of attendees filled the room. These folks, however, sat in a circle of chairs, chatting. Many held books in their hands. A woman glanced in Ash's direction, and he quickly pushed the door closed. Ash trotted down the hall.

Sylvia Grayson's story wouldn't hold up to

closer scrutiny, Ash thought. She had left the manuscript in Ramon's care when securing it inside the hotel safe would have been immensely wiser. She also lied to the cop when she said she didn't know about the inactive security cameras.

Ash paused in his thinking, considering another alternative. What if she had told the truth? Could Ramon have held the information back from the conference president? If he did so, that meant the concierge lied to Ash. Why would Ramon do that when he'd already admitted to money problems? Clearly, the concierge envisioned a way out of his troubles by stealing the manuscript. Maybe asking Ash if he wanted to get involved was Ramon's way of pushing himself over any final reservations. Ash needed to talk with the conference president so he could solidify his opinion on her involvement.

He stopped at the next door and opened it slightly. Tables covered by white clothes were spread around the room. Isaiah Grant hurried about, setting dishes in front of the unoccupied chairs. He looked toward the door and noticed Ash.

"Gimme a hand with this," he said. "Pizzas are on the way."

"Can't." Ash pushed the door a little wider. "I'm on a mission. Sorry."

"You're sorry?" Isaiah tossed a plate onto a table. It wobbled for a moment before losing steam. "I've gotta feed the conference, then clean up after them. All by myself."

Ash didn't want to lie and say he'd be back to help. He could cut through this room since only the chef was there. However, he would feel guilty not helping the man. It was a newer emotion, one he never felt with the Dawgs.

The only course of acceptable action seemed to close the door. Ash didn't feel like a good man at that moment, but more important matters demanded his attention. He hurried down the hall.

Nadine Delacroix also had some explaining to do when Ash caught up with her. The hotel manager spoke privately with Ramon, then left the storage room with something heavy in her purse. When she next appeared, she acted as if she was just arriving at the hotel. Her actions were highly suspicious. Unfortunately, only Ash seemed to have noticed her behavior.

Where did she go after talking with Ramon? Did she meet with anyone? What happened to the item she carried? If she indeed stole the manuscript, what did she do with it? Could she have slipped it under Ash's bed?

He opened another meeting door and peeked inside. More conference attendees clustered together. They seemed to be having a nice conversation as many were smiling and laughing. Before any of them could look his way, Ash quietly closed the door.

The final person he hoped to find was Hubert Dunn. Ash had several questions for the maintenance man. First, why had Hubie stopped responding to the radio calls? Second, why did he leave the hotel room open on the third floor? Finally, did Hubie still have his hammer—the one banging on his leg when he left the basement earlier?

Ash stopped at the final meeting room. One other door remained, this one at the end of the corridor. Unfortunately, it led into the gathering area. That's where he and Thelma had been earlier. A plethora of conference attendees likely waited out there.

He opened the door to the last meeting room and peered in. Vivienne Hart, the author in the tight red dress, spoke with Enoch and Loretta Mayfield. Loretta appeared delighted about the moment while her husband seemed clearly put out.

A large poster board stood on a three-legged display stand. Ash saw the white backing but couldn't see what was on the front. Vivienne's art portfolio case leaned against one of the stand's legs.

The romance author turned toward the door and her expression widened with curiosity.

Ash closed the door. He should turn around, head back to the assembly room where Isaiah was setting up the tables. Being seen by a friendly chef was better than getting noticed by conference attendees.

At the far end of the corridor, the entry door swung wide. A heavyset police officer stepped into the corridor. He noticed Ash immediately. "You!" he shouted. "Come here!"

Ash yanked open the door to the nearest

room and stepped in. The Mayfields spun toward him. Vivenne Hart's eyebrows rose with additional wonder.

"Speak of the devil," Enoch said. "The waiter."

Loretta excitedly pointed at Ash. "See, Vivienne? I told you."

"I saw him, too," Vivienne said. Her voice was sultry, a breathless whisper in a lover's ear.

As he passed the three-legged stand, Ash glanced at the poster. It looked like an oversized book. *The Clues of Temptation* was splashed across its top in bold, block letters. On the bottom, in a thinner, less obtrusive font, were the words *Vivienne Hart.*

Ash stopped walking, and his jaw dropped as recognition set in.

In the middle of the cover stood a muscular man. His white long-sleeve shirt was ripped open to expose tanned, well-defined pectorals. His long, dark hair flowed in the breeze. The man embraced a red-haired woman in his arms. Her ankle-length dress barely contained her ample assets. A European village burned in the background.

The cover model bore a striking resemblance to Ash if he didn't have tattoos, had long hair again, spent a summer in the sun, and lived in the Victorian era. Ash cocked his head.

"Look at him," Enoch said with a snicker. "Like a dog looking in a mirror."

Loretta nodded. "A spitting image if I ever saw one."

Vivienne smiled. "I'm at a loss for words."

Ash wanted to spend a couple of minutes understanding why he was on the cover of a romance mystery, but he didn't have time. The door to the service corridor opened and the overweight cop burst into the room.

"Don't move!" the officer shouted.

Ash didn't listen. He ran to the opposite side of the room.

"Stop!" the officer yelled. "Police!"

He kept moving. Stopping now wasn't a choice. Not since the cops found the manuscript under his temporary bed.

Ash stepped into the main hallway, turned left, and sprinted.

Chapter 12

Ash ran south through the conference center, hopping out of the way to avoid colliding with clustered guests. Many watched him rush by. Some even pointed.

Behind him, the heavyset cop wheezed, "Stop."

Ash raced into the gathering area. A group of Mystery Mavens were there. Their bright yellow shirts were beacons in a melting pot of blues, grays, and browns. He didn't bother to see if he recognized any of them.

They couldn't help his situation right now. He was being pursued and needed to put distance between himself and the cop. Ash knew a hard reality—it's nearly impossible to outrun a police radio. The officer might have called for help, which meant Ash's choices for escape were limited.

He grabbed the stairwell door and entered. Without hesitating, he ran up the stairs. Thelma Bennett's last call on the radio reported the cops had found the manuscript under his bed. Ash believed officers could still be in the basement, perhaps securing the area as a potential crime scene.

His legs burned as he ascended the stairs, two at a time. He passed the second floor and was halfway to the third when the door opened below.

"Stop," the heavyset cop gasped from below.

Ash took a couple more steps, then jumped onto the third-floor landing. He jerked open the door and entered the hallway. He sprinted toward the north end of the hotel, his legs and arms pumping. As he ran past room 308, a sliver of daylight shone through.

Someone had reopened the door and left it unlocked again.

He stopped running, an action that required several steps to come to a halt. Ash spun, hurried back to room 308 and stepped in. He shut the door and leaned against it.

Ash peered through the peephole. Several moments later, the bulky cop ran by, his weighty footsteps landing heavily on the carpet. The officer wheezed something into his radio, but Ash couldn't make it out from the other side of the door.

When the immediate danger faded down the hallway, Ash straightened and turned around.

Seated in the corner was Knuckles. His leather jacket lay on the bed. His hands were shoved into the front pocket of his hooded sweatshirt.

"Well, well, well," the enforcer said. "Look what the cat dragged in."

***

Ash never attended college. After high school,

everything he learned came from his time in the club. The Dawgs used to say their members were trained at The School of Hard Knocks with its campuses in every correctional institution, alleyway, or dive bar. The Art of Persuasion and Negotiation was a class always in session. A stranger's hard stare, puffed chest, or growing sneer was an introduction to that day's lesson.

Often, the threat of violence was enough to reach a desired result, whatever that may be. Other times required a fist, a knife, or a gun to bring about a compromise. Ash's former self was an excellent student at Hard Knocks.

The big man lounging in the wingback chair, one leg crossed over the other, seemed to have attended the same university. Even though they were both Hard Knocks alumni, there was no camaraderie between the two men.

"What're you doing here?" Ash said.

Knuckles casually glanced about the room. "I ain't baking a cake."

"How'd you get in here?"

"Call me Houdini."

"Someone let you in," Ash said. "I want to know who and why."

Knuckles scoffed. "Look at you, playing detective."

Ash crossed his arms but didn't speak.

"Maybe I found it open," Knuckles said.

"You didn't."

The thug smirked. "How do you know? I could have."

Ash dropped his arms by his sides. "I'm not

asking again."

"Then push off. I'm busy." The tough guy remained relaxed and apparently calm.

"We can do this the hard way," Ash said.

Knuckles scoffed as he pulled his hands free from the pocket of his sweatshirt. "Look at you. Not even offering an easy way."

"That's because there is no easy way."

"You're like a suburban guard dog." Knuckles smiled. "All bark and no bite."

"The cops want to talk with you."

"The cops?" Knuckles spread his arms wide. "What'd I do? I'm just sitting here."

"You killed Ramon." Ash didn't fully believe his accusation. However, he wanted to keep the enforcer talking until he figured out what was occurring.

Knuckles leaned forward; confusion played across his face. "Ramon's dead? How?"

That wasn't quite the reaction Ash expected. "He's dead because you killed him," he said, doubling down on the half-hearted claim.

"Me?"

"With a hammer." Ash mimed the killing motion.

"Don't pin no murder on me, pal." Knuckles dropped his hands on the chair's arms and pulled himself upright. "Why would I kill one of Mr. Leo's pigeons?"

Ash scowled. Ramon might have been a sucker, someone who lost consistently yet continued to bet, but Ash didn't like Knuckles talking about his friend that way.

"I wouldn't kill him." The enforcer tapped a finger into his open palm. "Dead men can't pay what's owed."

"Maybe you made him an example, so your other clients would know what's good for them."

"I make an example with a broken nose. Maybe some broken fingers. Killing a customer is bad business."

"You and I both know that's not true."

"What do you know?" Knuckles flicked his hand in Ash's direction. "You're a waiter. You know nothing."

"I know a detective who wants to talk with you." It was a lie. The cops didn't know about Knuckles since Ash hadn't told them.

The enforcer frowned. "The cops are really downstairs?"

"Investigating a murder takes time."

Knuckles studied his hands and remained silent.

"You didn't know about Ramon?" Ash asked.

"How could I?" The enforcer pointed at the floor. "I've been here waiting."

"How long?"

"Since I saw you."

That wasn't true. Ash and Thelma Bennett had been in this room shortly after Ramon's body was discovered. Knuckles wasn't here then. Maybe he was involved in Ramon's murder.

"Who let you in this room?" Ash asked.

"Give it a rest, Columbo," Knuckles said. The enforcer dropped back into the chair. He screwed a smile on and tried to appear unconcerned. Unfortunately for Knuckles, he wouldn't win a Best Actor award for this performance.

"You're not talking?" Ash asked.

"Take it on the road."

"Ramon's dead. You've got no reason to hang around. His debt is canceled."

Knuckles shrugged. "Maybe I rented this room."

"You didn't," Ash said. "The room is reserved for a guest arriving tomorrow."

"That so?"

Ash nodded. "Which means someone let you in. I want to know who."

"Mr. Detective." Knuckles pulled himself upright again. "Searching for clues without a magnifying glass."

Something occurred to Ash then, a partially formed thought, but Knuckles interrupted his process.

"Hit the bricks, princess."

Ash balled his fists. "I want some answers."

"Stop it." The enforcer grinned maliciously. "You're scaring me."

"Last chance." Ash stepped forward, closing the distance between the two men.

"Easy, fella," Knuckles said, holding up a hand. "Don't write a check your body can't cash."

"Talk or fight."

The thug leaped forward with a looping roundhouse punch. Ash brought his hands up and deflected the strike as he backpedaled several steps.

Knuckles swung a second and third time—both swinging blows. The enforcer leaned awkwardly forward to reach his retreating target.

Ash stopped abruptly and jabbed, connecting with his pursuer's face. It felt like punching a concrete wall. Knuckles paused briefly, allowing Ash time to throw a second strike—an uppercut. This one landed on the enforcer's chin, another blow against a concrete wall.

Knuckles remained upright and apparently unaffected by Ash's strikes. The enforcer juked by waggling his shoulders and shaking his head. He jumped forward, tackling Ash onto a small desk. Neither man fell to the floor.

Ash hit Knuckles in the head with an elbow. It barely rocked the enforcer, so he hit him again. The second blow also had little effect.

Knuckles let go of Ash, pushed slightly back, then slugged him in the gut. Ash saw the punch coming and tried to tighten his stomach muscles in preparation for the blow, but he was too late. He exhaled heavily before staggering backward toward the door.

Ash needed to catch his breath, but Knuckles followed him. The enforcer shimmied his shoulders, the way a cocky boxer does as he stalks an opponent across the ring. Knuckles threw a lazy jab to the left side of Ash's face. The arm remained extended, dangling the enforcer's fist precariously close to Ash's eye.

An inexperienced fighter might fall for the decoy strike, meant to encourage an opponent to move away, likely ducking low and to the right. If Ash took the bait, Knuckles would throw a thundering roundhouse to the right side of his head.

However, Ash wasn't inexperienced. His time in the Satan's Dawgs ensured he'd been in more than his share of fistfights. Therefore, he didn't react to the lackadaisical feint. Instead, Ash threw a right cross, straight and true, into the leaning enforcer's nose.

It was yet another blow into a concrete wall. This time, Knuckles's legs buckled, and the man dropped his hands. Ash hooked his next punch, catching the enforcer on the chin. Knuckles staggered backward until he collapsed onto the edge of the bed. He lay there for a moment before slowly spilling off and crumbling heavily on the carpeted floor.

It was then Ash heard a loud pounding from the neighboring room. Someone repeatedly hit the shared wall.

"Knock it off!" a man hollered. *Boom.* Another hand hit the wall. "I've called the front desk!" *Boom. Boom.* "They're sending up the cops!"

Ash pulled a wallet from the unconscious man's pocket. He opened it and checked the driver's license—Joseph K. Marino, with an address in the neighboring city of Brunswick.

Who let the thug into the room? There weren't many who could have done that—not today with so many out sick. Ash wanted to ponder the situation, but he couldn't stay in the room much longer.

If the neighbor in the next room really called the front desk, the police on scene were surely on the way. A brawl in the hotel was too much of a coincidence after a theft and a murder. The cop who pursued Ash only moments ago might still be in a stairwell. At worst, he got off on a different floor but was still nearby. The officer could be there in seconds.

Ash backed out of the room, looked left and right to make sure the coast was clear, and sprinted toward the furthest stairwell at the north end of the building.

Chapter 13

Ash yanked open the door and stepped into the stairwell. He paused long enough to listen for the sound of oncoming cops. The stairwell was silent except for the blood pounding in his ears.

He took a tentative step down, prepared to turn and run up the stairwell if any danger presented itself.

To where, though? The fourth, fifth, or sixth floor?

The proverbial walls were closing around him now. A cop spotted him in the kitchen corridor and chased him into a stairwell. Now, a guest likely reported his fight with Knuckles. It wouldn't take much for Detective Landry to put those pieces together.

Ash moved downward again, taking two steps in a single stride, his ears straining for anyone else moving in the stairwell.

He'd been wrongfully arrested for burglary while living in California under a different name. Luckily, the FBI agent who started this whole mess was vacationing nearby. He rescued the man Ash had been.

No help was coming now. Not unless someone reviewed abandoned calls on the marshal's emergency hotline. If a supervisor was monitoring, why hadn't they interrupted the computer operator? The government was not built with a customer-service mindset. Ash knew he had no right to expect the marshal service to act contrary to established norms.

He hurried as fast as silence would allow until he reached the second-floor landing. He paused and listened for several heartbeats. If someone burst into the stairwell from the first floor, Ash had options. He could climb higher, or he could enter the second floor.

If the cops caught Ash, surely Detective Landry would assume he was involved in Ramon's murder. The circumstantial evidence pointed in Ash's direction. Ash admitted to knowing the missing manuscript was valuable. He also admitted to being in the center stairwell, just moments before the discovery of Ramon's body.

Perhaps most damning was the shoddy job prepping the Asher Reed background. Both the marshal service and Ash shared some blame in that matter. Lester Krumland hadn't planned for a nosy detective. Traffic infractions for a man without a car were bad enough. Not knowing the make of the vehicle sank Ash's story, and it was something he could have easily studied and learned.

He stepped down quietly. One step, then a second.

If Detective Landry caught and arrested Ash, would Krumland come and get him? He would, but who knew what would happen to Ash afterward. He'd likely not get reassigned anywhere.

Ash inhaled deeply before rushing down to the first-floor landing. It was a risky decision. A cop could be on the other side of the door. If one wasn't standing guard, they might be roaming the north hallway.

He grabbed the door handle, steeling himself to jump out of the frying pan and into the fire.

The radio on his hip beeped once. A barely audible call came through channel 4. *"Miss Marple to Hercule. Are you there?"*

Ash pulled the device from his belt. Its screen was lit a bright orange. Before he could respond, Thelma Bennett transmitted again. *"You won't believe it,"* she said. *"We found your cat."*

Travis, Ash thought. He mentally sighed a breath of relief. Finding the little guy removed one problem from his plate. He lifted the radio to his lips, but it beeped again, switching to channel 5.

"We found him," Estelle Enderby said. *"The Mavens did."*

The radio switched to channel 4, chirping as it did so. *"That's not true,"* Thelma said. *"We found the kitty at the same time."*

Ash examined the radio. There had to be a way to stop the device from beeping. The audible alert never bothered Ash while in the course of his job. However, when hiding in a stairwell from the cops, the beep was the worst thing he could imagine.

The radio chirped again, and Estelle

transmitted, "*Fine. We found the cat at the same time.*"

He thought he discovered how to quiet the beep. A small speaker with a line through it was above the light button. Ash pressed the function key and the light button. Nothing happened.

"*Hercule?*" Estelle asked. No beep corresponded with the transmission and the screen remained dark.

He lifted the radio to his lips. "*That's great news,*" he whispered. "*Where is he?*"

"*Well,*" Thelma said, "*that's a bit of a problem.*"

Ash backed up the stairs to the second-floor landing, worried a police officer might burst through the stairwell with all the chattering and beeping.

"Why's that a problem?" he transmitted.

"*Two women have him and won't surrender poor, little Travis,*" Estelle said.

"Who?"

"*One of them is Carrie Fenton,*" Thelma added. "*I'm not sure about the other.*"

Daphne Winterbourne, Ash thought. He tried to respond, but the radio switched to channel 5.

"*She's a true crime author,*" Estelle said. "*Carrie Fenton. Not the other one.*"

"*I've read her true-crime work,*" Thelma said. "*You're lucky if she's involved in this mystery. The crime will get solved soon.*"

"*She reports crimes,*" Estelle said. "*She doesn't solve them.*"

When there was a break in the back-and-forth, Ash pressed the transmission button. He was on channel 4. "Where are they?"

"*In the lobby,*" Thelma said. "*Right next to the fountain.*"

"*Next to a bunch of ankle biters,*" Estelle added.

The radio switched to channel 4. "*We told them we've been trying find Mister Snuglewhiskers and return him to you, but they won't let us have him. What should we tell them?*"

Ash responded, "I'll handle it."

"*What's our next move, Hercule?*"

"You're breaking up," Ash said. He switched off the radio then.

Standing in the stairwell was too much of a risk. He needed to find a safer place to think. Maybe then he could figure out how to get Travis, talk with Daphne, and solve Ramon's murder.

Ash clipped the silenced radio to his belt as he returned to the first-floor landing. He opened the door, made sure no cops were around, and stepped into the north hallway.

***

The hotel's restaurant, coffee shop, and convenience store were in the north wing of the hotel. A workout room and swimming pool were also down this wing. The corridor bent slightly, obscuring a straight view of the lobby.

The overhead lights were softer in this section

of the hotel. Murals of ocean scenes were painted on the walls between the shops and hotel amenities.

Construction paper blocked the windows of Marlowe's at Bayside. The restaurant sat at the farthest end of the north corridor, giving patrons an unobstructed view of the Atlantic Ocean. A sign outside the establishment read, *Pardon our dust. Exciting changes are coming!*

Ash was about to pass the restaurant when he decided to peek inside. The entry door was unlocked, and he entered. No one was inside the space, which wasn't a surprise. All construction had stopped on Marlowe's at Bayside since most of the crew had come down with the flu, too.

The exciting changes the hotel promised were a discrete change in paint color, replaced hardwood flooring, and different tables and chairs. Supposedly, the menu remained the same as did the employee uniforms.

He took a final glance around before leaving.

Ash passed Java Haven next. A line of waiting customers flowed from the order counter into the hallway. Only one barista seemed to be working now. She dashed from the espresso machine to the cash register and back. Those waiting seemed to be irritated by the long delay. The folks sitting at tables weren't in any hurry to leave.

On the other side of the hallway was the pool. He imagined it was full of parents and screaming kids. That's how it had been in the past. However, Ash couldn't see in because the window tint protected the privacy of those swimming.

The fitness facility, however, was like a fishbowl. All inside were on display while they lifted weights, ran on a treadmill, or rode an exercise bike. Ash thought it strange to leave the windows unshaded. Was it because the owners of the hotel wanted to encourage their guests to get in shape? Or did those same owners want its healthy guests to become jealous by the good time other guests were having doing anything else?

Ash slowed as he neared the corridor's bend. He could see the windows of Grab & Go Depot, the hotel's one-stop shop. Ahead and still out of sight was the lobby. Before reaching it was the center stairwell where Ash suspected several cops lingered, protecting the crime scene.

He was about to back away from the bend when he noticed Nadine Delacroix inside the convenience store. She stood near the farthest window, her attention drawn in the lobby's direction. The manager held a tissue in front of her face as if preparing for a sneeze. However, the relief never arrived, and her hands remained steady as a makeshift mask.

Ash glanced over his shoulder to make sure no cops were around, then he dashed into the shop.

Nadine didn't notice his entry, but the older woman behind the counter did. Over the past weeks, Ash had developed a friendly relationship with Marlene Johnson. He swung into the store almost daily since he never packed a lunch.

Marlene smiled and waved. He returned the gesture but didn't head in her direction. Instead, he approached the hotel's manager.

"The cops are looking for you," he whispered.

Nadine jumped and dropped the hands and tissue from her face. She was in her late thirties, with jet black hair and green eyes. The same beige, slouchy purse hung over her right shoulder. Nadine looked every bit professional, except for the bag and the redness at the tip of her nose, a tell-tale sign of her illness.

"They're looking for you, too," she said, stuffy. Her gaze swept back to the lobby area.

From where they stood, Ash could see the center stairwell. Two cops guarded the crime scene. Detective Landry wasn't anywhere. Ramon's lifeless body was likely still on the first-floor landing. It had only been a short time since his discovery. Certainly no one had arrived yet to whisk away the body.

Nadine lifted the tissue to her nose and blew. She stuffed the used material into her purse and pulled a clean tissue out. She lifted it to her face, preparing for a blow that never came. Her cold made for a convenient disguise.

Ash studied her eyes now. They were puffy and red. Caused by her cold, or could she have been crying? He couldn't tell.

She lifted an elbow toward the lobby. "A slew of cops took off a few minutes ago. Looked like they were chasing someone." Her gaze cut to

Ash. "You?"

"Maybe."

"Why are they after you?"

"They suspect I'm involved in Ramon's death."

Nadine pulled back, suddenly concerned about her proximity to Ash. The lower portion of her face remained hidden behind the tissue she held, but it couldn't hide the concern in her eyes. "Were you?"

"No."

Her gaze lingered on him for a moment longer until she returned her attention down the hallway. "What's stopping me from going over there and reporting you?"

"You're hiding, too."

Nadine eyed him. "Maybe I don't want to get involved."

"You're the manager. It's your job to get involved."

"Murder wasn't listed in my job description." She continued to study the crime scene.

The cops standing outside the center stairwell chatted casually with each other. Occasionally, one of them laughed. The dead man lying a few feet away was an ordinary distraction, nothing to put a damper on a good story, whatever it may be.

Ash asked, "What was going on with you and Ramon?"

Nadine blew her nose. "Nothing."

"There was something."

She wadded the tissue and put it in her

purse, then pulled out a clean one and held it in front of her face. "Whatever you're after, you're barking up the wrong tree."

"I don't think I am. I watched you go into the storage room. Saw Ramon there, too. He looked worried."

The manager's eyes slid toward him; the tissue she held still masked the lower portion of her face. "If he was worried, it wasn't because of me."

Ash wasn't getting the answers he wanted, so he went straight at her. "I saw you take the manuscript from the storage room." He motioned at her purse. "You put it in there and walked right out."

Nadine's hands lowered now, and a frown creased her lips. "You're not leaving, are you?"

"Not until I get some answers."

The manager's shoulders slumped. "Fine." She turned, walked to the rear of the shop, and stopped at the counter. Ash followed her.

Marlene stopped refilling the candy shelf and looked up.

Nadine jerked her thumb toward the storeroom. "We're stepping in the back."

"Ma'am?"

"Counseling session." Nadine didn't wait for a response. She entered the storeroom.

Marlene cringed as she eyed Ash. "Good luck," she whispered.

***

The stockroom was like others Ash had been in. Unfinished walls framed the small area. Lightbulbs hung exposed from the ceiling. Boxes of products stacked at various heights clogged the walkway.

Unused promotional signs lay on top of several containers, promising deals for candy, books, and packaged hardboiled eggs.

In the far corner was a door to the rear of the hotel. Ash knew Marlene used it to sneak out to the boardwalk and smoke a cigarette during her breaks. If he wanted, Ash could simply walk away from the entire day by taking that exit. However, that wasn't the action a good man would take.

"What is it you want, Ash?" Nadine sat on a large box with her purse resting on her lap. "Can't you see I'm busy?"

Ash studied the hotel manager for a moment. Her eyes never cut toward the exit. She had no interest in slipping out the back, either.

"Who planned the heist?" Ash asked. "You or Ramon?"

"Heist?"

"The manuscript."

Nadine scoffed. "Why would I steal some dusty book?"

"So you knew what it was?"

"Whatever." She waved her hand. "I know what a manuscript is."

"He tell you it was valuable?"

She rolled her eyes. "You're out of your mind with this."

"I know what I saw, Nadine, and I saw it in your purse."

Ash hadn't seen the manuscript. He only saw her purse suddenly heavy, banging against her hip as she walked. If she didn't take the manuscript, she'd deny it or tell him what she put in her purse.

Nadine pulled out a tissue and blew her nose. When she finished, she dropped her hands into her lap. "I didn't kill Ramon. I liked him."

"You took the manuscript, though."

"Stop accusing me. You got no proof."

Ash crossed his arms. "Why'd you take it? Do you have money troubles like Ramon?"

Nadine stuffed the used tissue into her purse. "Ramon told you about his losses?"

"Some."

"Some losses? More like lots of losses." Nadine grabbed a promotional poster and feigned reading it. "He tell you some thug was looking for him?"

"Joseph Marino," Ash said.

"Joey. That's him." Nadine pushed the poster away. It slipped off the nearby box and floated to the floor. "Ramon laid it out for you, I guess."

"He didn't tell me much. I figured it out after I met Marino."

Nadine's eyes narrowed. "Joey was here? Before or after Ramon's murder?"

"Both."

"Okay, okay." Nadine nodded several times. "Then we've got it solved. Joey murdered Ramon because of an owed debt. Simple." She hopped to her feet. "Let's tell the police."

"He didn't kill Ramon."

"Sure, he did."

"He didn't," Ash said.

She cast a sideways glance. "How can you be sure?"

"He's still in the hotel."

"What's he doing now?"

"Snoring. I knocked him unconscious on the third floor."

Nadine returned to her seat. She studied Ash for several moments. "You think Joey rented a room for an alibi? So if he got in trouble, he'd have a reason to be in the hotel?"

"He didn't rent the room. Someone let him in."

"Who?"

"I was thinking maybe it was you."

"Me?" Nadine's face darkened. "Why would I let him in?"

"I don't know. Maybe he was part of the manuscript theft."

"Where's your proof?"

"I'm working on it."

Nadine looked toward the ceiling. "What was Joey doing on the third floor?"

"Waiting to get paid."

"But Ramon is dead."

"He didn't know. I figured he was waiting for Ramon to bring him the money."

"Ramon didn't have any money," Nadine said. "He was broke."

"You were cutting him in on the heist."

"Stop with that."

"Maybe Ramon was going to double-cross you."

Nadine inhaled deeply. "You do this often? Play detective. Is that like a hobby of yours or something?"

"Ramon asked me if I wanted to steal it."

"What for?" Nadine asked.

"Maybe he wanted a better deal."

She leaned forward and rested her elbows on her knees. "You're really bad at this detective gig."

Ash continued. "You and Ramon were going to steal the manuscript, but he didn't like the terms you guys had. So he offered to steal it with me for a better split."

Nadine pursed her lips. "Joey is still on the third floor?"

"Why? You thinking of selling the manuscript to him?"

"I don't think Mr. Leo is into collecting manuscripts. I was just wondering."

"Changing the subject."

Nadine shrugged. "Says you."

Ash leaned on a tower of cardboard boxes. "It's time to come clean, Nadine. Tell me why you stole the manuscript."

She clucked. "You need a calculator, Sherlock. Your clues aren't adding up."

"What was in your purse?"

Nadine lowered her gaze until it landed on her bag. Her eyes bounced back to him. "Tissues. I had a box of tissues."

"Not with how heavy your purse looked."

The hotel manager stood. "I don't know what to tell you."

"Here's what I think."

"Oh, do tell," Nadine interrupted. "I can't wait to hear this."

"There's someone else in this heist."

She scoffed. "Stop calling it a heist."

"You and Sylvia Grayson are friends."

"What's that got to do with anything?" She reached into her purse for another tissue.

"Maybe everything. One of the conference attendees told me. That's why the mystery readers' conference moved here. Sylvia got on the board, and you gave them a deal to switch venues."

"So?" Nadine blew her nose. "That's good business."

"Maybe it was the building block of the entire heist."

"The heist, the heist." Nadine threw her hands in the air. "What is it with you?"

"An unknown party sent the manuscript to the hotel." Ash's eyes narrowed. "Who wrote it, by the way?"

"Why's it matter?"

He shrugged. "I guess it doesn't. What matters is it was considered valuable, and someone stole it because of that. They maybe even murdered Ramon for it."

"Hold on," Nadine said. "You're jumping to conclusions. Maybe the theft had nothing to do with the murder."

"Maybe it didn't," Ash said. "Maybe it did.

Here's some more I've learned. Sylvia knows who wrote the manuscript, how valuable it is, and that it was supposed to be auctioned off on Saturday."

"And?"

"She refused to secure it in the hotel safe, instead opting to leave it in the concierge's storage room, making it an easy target for a theft."

"Sounds like you should be talking with Sylvia."

"You're the one who walked into the concierge office and took it."

Nadine tsked. "You're off your rocker."

"I don't think I am," Ash said. "What I want to know is why you hid the manuscript under the rollaway bed in the basement?"

"I don't know what you're talking about."

"That's okay. The cops found it."

Nadine's expression darkened. Her lips twisted, then her tongue darted out and wet her lips. "It's a fine story, but we're done here."

"That's how it's going to be?"

"Yeah," Nadine said. "That's how it's going to be. I don't know anything, I haven't seen anything, and I'm not saying anything."

"Yet you're hiding out here with your guilty conscience."

The hotel manager smirked. "We're hiding here together."

"Not anymore."

Ash headed for the door.

"Where are you going?"

"To get to the bottom of this."
"In that case," Nadine said. "You're fired."

Chapter 14

Ash left the convenience store like a thief slipping into the shadows. He glanced toward the center stairwell but couldn't see it because of the hallway's curvature. He headed in the opposite direction.

The coffee shop line remained long as the sole barista struggled to stay up with demand. Those waiting barely noticed Ash as he hurried by.

He stole glances over his shoulder to make sure no one followed. Ash continued until he reached Marlowe's at the Bay. He opened the door and stepped into the quiet restaurant. The windows facing the hallway were covered but the exterior windows were open. Ash walked over to a booth and sat. Dust covered the table. His mind raced as he sorted through everything he'd learned.

Ash believed Nadine and Sylvia conspired to steal the manuscript. Nadine likely helped because of friendship, but why did Sylvia want the manuscript? Could it be as simple as greed? Did she have money problems like Ramon? Perhaps there was another motivation for the theft.

He wanted to talk with the conference president, but how could he find her without attracting the cops? Ash pulled his radio from his belt and turned it on. Immediately, someone called. He was happy he had turned off the beeping signal.

"*Hercule?*" Thelma Bennett asked. "*Where are you?*"

Ash pressed the transmit button. "I'm here, Miss Marple."

"*Wonderful. You're okay. I was getting worried.*"

"Are you alone?"

"*Mostly,*" Thelma whispered. "*A couple of the Mavens are nearby. Some other readers, too.*" Her voice grew softer. "*And the cops.*"

"Where are you?"

"*In the lobby.*"

"Any news to report?"

"*Unfortunately, yes,*" Thelma said. "*Your kitty got away.*"

"From Daphne?"

"*Is that the woman with Carrie Fenton? Then, yes. He jumped right out of her hands and scampered away. Most of my group went after him. Some of the Mavens, too.*"

"Where's Daphne now?"

"*She's with the detective investigating the murder. Carrie Fenton, too.*"

"He already talked with them."

"*I know. I think he's holding them to lure you out. They're at the fountain now. Several policemen are around them, trying to look nonchalant, but they're in their uniforms.*"

Ash bowed his head. He never wanted to drag Daphne into his troubles. For that matter, he didn't want to pull Carrie in, either. Perhaps he should turn himself in now. Just go to the lobby and answer Detective Landry's questions.

Even though he'd met a dirty cop or two in his life, Ash didn't get that feeling from Landry. He still wasn't sure about the investigator's competency. Integrity didn't guarantee proficiency.

Holding Daphne and Carrie as bait was not the same as charging them with a crime. It was inconvenient. Maybe even slightly embarrassing. Yet both would survive.

"*Hercule?*" Thelma transmitted. "*Still there?*"

"*Yes,*" Ash said. He drew a circle in the dust on the table. "*Just thinking.*"

"*Have you learned anything about your friend's death?*"

"*Some. There are still missing pieces.*" He put two dots in the upper portion of the circle.

"*Can I help?*"

"I need to talk with Sylvia."

"*Grayson? The conference president? Why?*"

"I need some answers about the manuscript." Ash dragged his finger through the dirt, creating a curved line under the two dots. "Do you know where she is?"

"*Sylvia's talking with Estelle and Maxine. I don't know where the rest of the group is.*"

"Can you bring her to me?"

"*Guess that depends on where you are.*"

Ash drew two triangles on the top of the circle. A smiling cat grinned up at him.

"The closed restaurant," Ash said.

"Where?"

"Marlowe's at the Bay but be discrete about it."

"Copy, Hercule. Over and out."

***

Ash stood near an outside window overlooking the ocean. Underneath a sky grayed by clouds, the waves hypnotically rolled in and out. A flock of birds flew above the water, using the slight breeze to aid in their hovering. Ash hadn't been outside since his day started, but the temperature was likely chilly.

This was the second time Ash lived near the Atlantic Ocean. The other was his first Witness Protection assignment in Pleasant Valley, Maine. He didn't appreciate the ocean much while up north. He was still dealing with new feelings of being in the program. It also took some time for him to realize citizens were different when he wasn't wearing a Satan's Dawgs' cut.

He unbuttoned the burgundy vest and tossed it on a nearby table. If he was indeed fired, there wasn't a requirement to wear the porter's uniform. He unfastened his cuffs and rolled them up, exposing the tattoos on his forearms.

A group of children played on the beach while their smiling parents stood clustered together on the boardwalk. Parents were the same everywhere, Ash thought. Procreate, then pat themselves on the backs for their lack of foresight.

Ash had taken many walks along the boardwalk since his arrival. When families weren't clogging the path, it was a nice way to clear his mind and be alone with his thoughts. He was under no illusions today. He'd likely never get to stroll the path again now that trouble had found him.

Trouble remained constant in Ash's life, whether it was with the motorcycle club or while in the Witness Protection Program.

When trouble found him with the Dawgs, it was his own doing. Ash's former self willfully violated the law and acted selfishly in non-criminal matters. He associated with known offenders, an act prosecuting attorneys mentioned repeatedly whenever Ash found himself on trial. It wasn't a surprise when trouble found him, then. It was an expected fact of life.

Ash thought life might change for the better when he entered the Witness Protection Program. Yet, he'd been dodging trouble since he left Leavenworth prison.

Bad acts have a habit of returning to their source, his grandmother used to say. One of the club's hang-around girls called it karma. Ash didn't know what to believe, except he wasn't behaving badly anymore. He wanted to be a better man and was trying to act accordingly.

Shouldn't that account for something? Shouldn't the universe reward him for striving toward a goal?

The flock of birds moved over the beach, diving occasionally to scavenge something from the sand. A boy in a red baseball cap chased a momentarily grounded tern until it took flight, abandoning its treasure.

Ash no longer wanted to see the bookkeeper in his mirror. Someone better lived inside him. Ash was certain of it. That man just had to work his way out.

He also wanted to be a man worthy of his grandmother's love. Ash wished he could call her, but that was dangerous for them both. The Dawgs might have her under surveillance, watching her routine, maybe even listening to her phone calls. The FBI agent who convinced Ash to turn against the club said the agency would monitor her. He believed that was true.

Then there was Daphne. Ash wanted to be a better man for her. It was a silly desire, he knew. They only spent a short time together while he was in Pleasant Valley, but that was all he needed. Their kiss cemented his devotion, something he had never before experienced.

However, Ash knew they should never be together. There couldn't be a happily ever after ending. It was an unfortunate truth his past dictated. Yet here she was in a coastal Georgia town, over a thousand miles from where they first met and months away from the time they shared.

Perhaps it was fate, a concept Ash would usually dismiss. If his troubles were a result of karma, perhaps Daphne's arrival was the universe's way of rewarding his attempts at bettering himself?

If that were true, then why had Carrie Fenton popped into his life twice since he left Pleasant Valley? He held no affection for her beyond simple friendship. What was fate trying to do with her?

His brow furrowed as he tried to recall how the two women knew each other. As far as he could recall, the two hadn't met while he worked at The Red Herring, Pleasant Valley's only mystery bookstore. He also didn't remember telling Carrie about Daphne while in Chicago.

Had the two women come together via the bookstore after his departure? That's where he met each of them, albeit at different times. The business had been owned by the U.S. Marshals. Would the government have sold it to a local operator?

A tern landed on the windowsill, directly in front of Ash. It had a black head, gray back, and white belly. Upon his arrival at Marlowe Bay, Ash called these birds seagulls. Ramon was the one who corrected him.

Ramon. Ash frowned as his thoughts jumped to the concierge.

When he asked if Ash would steal the manuscript with him, was Ramon already in league with Nadine? What about Sylvia?

Ash's scowl deepened. The conference president seemed surprised when Ash told Detective Landry that Nadine was in the hotel. Assuming the two women conspired to steal the manuscript, had Nadine double-crossed her friend?

Before he could ponder those questions any longer, the door to the restaurant opened.

***

Thelma Bennett smiled up at Ash as she patted his arm. "How are you doing, my boy?"

Standing next to her was Sylvia Grayson. Behind them were Estelle Enderby and Maxine Coleman.

"Him?" Sylvia said, her face pinched with disbelief. "This is the Hercule you wanted me to meet?"

Estelle harrumphed. "I still can't believe you nicknamed this joker."

"Don't you have code names?" Thelma asked. "I thought that's what people did on the radio."

"What's your code name?" Maxine asked.

"Miss Marple, of course."

Maxine's face brightened. "I want a code name."

"No," Estelle said, flatly.

"How about Tuppence Beresford?" Maxine said, her eyes widening with delight. "She's another Agatha Christie sleuth."

"I know," Thelma said, clapping. "It's perfect."

Estelle cleared her throat. "No. Definitely not."

"Because it's too long?" Maxine asked. "How about just Tuppence?

"Stow it, Maxie. Nobody's getting any more

codes names, especially not Tuppence.”

“All right, enough,” Sylvia said as she waved for the assembled women to quiet. “Someone tell me what he’s doing here.”

“Hercule and I are working together,” Thelma said proudly. “We’re investigating the theft of the manuscript and the concierge’s murder.”

“Wait.” Estelle held up her hand like a school crossing guard. “This joker is working with us.” She waggled her handheld radio as proof, then her eyes narrowed as she looked at Ash. “Have you been two-timing us?”

“Yeah,” Maxine chimed in. “Double-crosser.”

Ash suddenly felt guilty. He couldn’t put his finger on why. “I’m helping you both,” Ash said, which was stupid to say since he hadn’t intended on assisting either group.

“Helping us both?” Estelle scoffed. “I know guys like you.” She turned to Maxine. “Well, what do you think?”

“Well,” Maxine said with a shrug. “We really didn’t give him a choice, did we?”

Estelle stiffened. “You saying this is my fault?”

Sylvia raised her hands to stop the chatter. “Can we focus here?” Her gaze shifted to Thelma. “You said Vivienne Hart wanted to see me, not the porter.”

“I’m sorry.” Thelma shrugged. “It was a ruse.”

“Very nice,” Estelle said with an appreciative smile. “I didn’t think you had it in you.”

“Neither did I,” Thelma admitted. “This amateur sleuth work isn’t as hard as the books make out."

"Tell me about it." Estelle thumbed at Ash. "If we're relying on this joker, it's gotta be a piece of cake."

Ash's gaze bounced between the Mavens and the sole Bookworm. "You guys are friends now?"

"Call us reluctant allies," Estelle said. "Situation dependent."

Thelma motioned to the Mavens. "These two saw me talking with Sylvia and tagged along."

"I thought maybe she was getting an edge on this mystery," Estelle said. She faced Thelma with an apologetic smile. "Couldn't have that now, could we?"

Maxine cocked her head. "What about Warshawski?"

"What about it?" Estelle asked.

"For a code name."

Ash raised an eyebrow. He finally caught a reference, since he'd read one of Sara Paretsky's books. Even though he was trying to solve a murder, Ash felt oddly proud knowing about Chicago private investigator, V.I. Warshawski.

"We're past nicknames, Maxie. Let it go."

"Would be a good one, though," Thelma said.

Estelle clucked. "Think where this goes. If you get a nickname, Maxie, then I'll want one. So will all the other Mavens. Keeping everyone straight will be a nightmare."

"I guess," Maxine mumbled. "Still, it would have been neat."

Sylvia muttered a sharp expletive, which caused everyone to stop talking. "Can we pay attention now?"

"We could have done without that," Estelle said.

"Swearing is a sign of an undisciplined mind," Thelma added.

Ash's grandmother had taught him the same saying. Because of her, he didn't swear. Even while in the Dawgs, Ash never cursed. The other guys thought it odd, but they kept it to themselves. The club's bookkeeper was allowed to have his idiosyncrasies. Ash knitted to reduce stress, another skill taught to him by his grandmother. He never made anything, though; he simply knitted several lines, then stopped and pulled the line free. Only one Dawg thought teasing Ash's former self about his knitting was a good idea. That man had plenty of time to reconsider the error of his ways while getting his jaw rewired in the hospital.

Sylvia sighed. "I apologize for my outburst." She spun to Ash. "Why should I talk with you? You and Ramon stole the manuscript."

"I didn't steal anything," Ash said. "Besides, you were already planning to steal it."

Thelma and Maxine inhaled sharply while Sylvia stiffened. The conference president's gaze remained locked on Ash.

"Take that back," she said.

"You were planning to steal it with Nadine," Ash said.

Estelle leaned forward. "The hotel manager?" Estelle waved at Maxine. "Write that down."

Sylvia's eyes darkened and her lips twisted.

"You don't know what you're talking about."

"Sure, I do," Ash said. "You refused to put the manuscript in the hotel safe. Instead, you wanted it kept in the storage room where anyone had access to it."

"Not anyone," Sylvia said abruptly. "Just Ramon." As an afterthought, she added, "You, too, since you're the only porter working."

Estelle clucked. "Right when I think I'm liking the guy."

"Still seems odd," Thelma interjected, "that Sylvia didn't secure the manuscript better, especially since it's supposed to be valuable." She looked back at the Mavens. "Has someone told us how valuable it is?"

Estelle looked at Maxine, who checked her notebook. Before she could find the answer, Ash said, "Ten thousand."

"That's all?" Thelma asked.

"Look at you," Estelle said. "Miss Moneybags."

Maxine's eyes widened. "*Moneypenny!* I'll use that as my nickname."

Estelle rolled her eyes. "No."

Thelma waved a hand to get the attention of the Mavens. "What I'm saying is ten thousand seems like a small amount for all the risk."

Ash's gaze slid to Thelma. When he joined the Dawgs, he learned people stole for a variety of reasons. Money was only one of them. Hunger, thrill, and revenge were a few others.

"People steal for a lot less," Estelle said.

"Murder for less, too," Maxine suggested.

"Sure, they do," Thelma said, "but if Hercule thinks Sylvia worked with the manager to steal it, then I tend to agree with him." She turned to Ash. "Would they split the take fifty/fifty?"

"Maybe they'd go sixty/forty," Estelle said. "Whoever brings in the idea gets the lion's share."

Maxine nodded. "That's how they do it in the books."

"That's my point," Thelma said. "An equal split would only net them five thousand a piece. If Nadine was caught, she'd lose her job. I'm sure she makes a salary that's a lot more than her share of the take."

Ash furrowed his brow. Thelma made an excellent point. He hadn't weighed what the thief might gain from the theft against what they could lose if caught. Jail and prison were always at the forefront of his mind when he worked a job with the motorcycle club, but he never had to consider losing a job, a pension, or employment status. Dawgs, by nature, were unemployable.

"So." Maxine touched her chin as she thought. "What you're saying is the thief would have little to lose. Why else get involved?"

Estelle considered Ash. "How much do you make?"

He told her.

"That's all? Yipes." Estelle turned to Maxine. "What do you think?"

"I don't know." Maxine shrugged. "I'd probably steal the manuscript if that's all I made."

"Me, too," Estelle said. Her eyes narrowed as she studied Ash. "Maybe you took it."

The government provided Ash with a stipend to cover any costs that his paycheck didn't. So far, he lived small and didn't have any needs beyond the basics—which included cat food, litter, and jingle balls.

"I didn't steal the manuscript," Ash protested.

"Would you kill your friend to take it?" Estelle asked Maxine.

"You're my only friend," she said.

Estelle put her hands on her hips. "That wasn't an answer."

"If I made as much as Hercule, then maybe. Yeah, sure."

"Is that so?" Estelle pursed her lips. "I'm gonna keep my eye on you, Maxie."

Ash pointed at the conference president. "How'd you and Nadine decide to split the take?"

"What take?" Sylvia crossed her arms. "This whole thing is ridiculous. I'm leaving and telling the cops where to find you."

She didn't move, though. The conference president remained rooted where she stood.

"Are you worried Nadine betrayed you?" Ash asked.

"She wouldn't do that."

"Ah-ha!" Thelma exclaimed. "You were involved!"

Sylvia rolled her eyes. "I misspoke. Worrying about Nadine's action implies I planned to do something inappropriate."

"Illegal is more like it," Estelle said.

The conference president continued. "I didn't do anything of the sort."

"How much was the manuscript worth, really?" Ash asked.

Sylvia gnawed on her lower lip as her eyes drifted to a window. The flock of terns continued to hover above the beach, looking for their next treasure. A couple of seconds passed before Sylvia whispered, "A hundred thousand."

"Cha-ching," Thelma said. "A hundred Gs!"

Estelle shook her head in disbelief. "A hundred K."

Maxine whistled. "A hundred smackers."

Everyone turned to her, even Sylvia.

"What?" Maxine asked.

"That's a hundred bucks," Estelle said. "Not a hundred thousand."

Maxine appeared confused. "It's not? I've probably read a lot of books wrong, then."

Thelma shook her finger as she thought. "Who's attending the conference that could bid that much?"

"No one I know," Estelle said.

Something occurred to Maxine, and her expression widened with shock. "The manuscript was never going to make it to the auction block, was it?"

"We've established that," Estelle said. "Keep up, Maxie. Things are moving quickly now."

"You don't know what you're talking about," Sylvia said under her breath.

"Hold on," Thelma said. "We still don't know

who wrote the manuscript."

Sylvia sighed. "Not that it makes much difference, but it was written by—"

Ash's radio came alive. "*Ash,*" Finley called. His voice was quiet. "*If you hear this, call me back.*"

"Who's that?" Maxine asked.

"The desk clerk," Ash said.

Estelle frowned. "The shaky guy who gave away my room?"

"I thought he was very resourceful," Maxine said. "Exceptional customer service."

Thelma jumped, surprised by something unseen. "My phone is buzzing," she said and hurriedly pulled it from her pocket.

Ash removed the radio from his belt and keyed it. "I'm here, Finley. What's going on?"

"*The cops found Hubie.*"

"Is he okay?"

"Who's Hubie?" asked Maxine.

Estelle rolled her eyes. "A late addition to the mystery."

Thelma answered her phone, then turned away from the group. "Hello, honey," she said.

Finley's voice came through the radio again. "*We're in the lobby. Hubie's in handcuffs.*"

Ash keyed the microphone. "The cops think Hubie's involved?"

"*That's what it looks like.*"

Maxine waved at Ash. "Ask if anyone found your cat," she whispered.

"Stay focused," Estelle said. "This Hubie guy is going to be important."

"Are the cops still looking for me?" Ash asked.

Estelle and Maxine exchanged glances.

"Look who's got a big head," Estelle said. "Thinking this whole mess revolves around him."

Maxine clucked. "His kitty's safety seems a low priority."

"*Right now,*" Finley transmitted, "*the cops seem only focused on Hubie.*"

Ash didn't want to believe Hubie might be involved. Yes, the murder weapon was supposedly a hammer. Yes, Hubie was the only maintenance man working due to the flu outbreak. Yes, Hubie really didn't like Ramon, but he really didn't like any of the lobby folks. Besides, everyone had access to the basement. If Hubie was going to murder someone, Ash believed the guy would be smart enough to not use a tool the cops could easily link to him.

"I bet this one's a dog person," Estelle said, not bothered by Ash's disapproving look. "Him and Phyllis."

"He's not that bad," Maxine insisted.

"Even worse." Estelle's frown morphed into a scowl. "He looks like a big dog person."

"If he's anything like Ramon," Sylvia said, "he's a dirty dog. Girlfriends galore. I heard a rumor that he and Vivienne Hart had something."

Maxine's eyebrows shot up. "The porter and Vivienne? Is that how he got on the cover of her book?"

"No," Sylvia said. "Ramon."

Estelle rapidly shook her head. "The porter and Ramon? Now, I'm really confused."

Several steps away, Thelma said, "We'll see you in a couple of minutes." She turned around with a grin. "My daughter's here." As she walked back to the group, Thelma's gaze bounced from those assembled until it landed on Ash. "Wait until you meet Kinsey. You're gonna love her. She's a cutie."

Estelle jerked her thumb at Ash. "You want your daughter to meet this joker?"

"What's wrong with him?" Thelma asked, suddenly concerned. "I think he'd make a fine beau."

Ash raised an eyebrow but held his tongue.

"If you no longer need me," Sylvia said and stepped back. "My conference is going down in flames."

"Hold on." Ash clipped the radio back to his belt. "Convince us you didn't murder Ramon."

"Why should I do that?" Sylvia smirked. "The police have done that by arresting that Hubie fellow."

"I still don't know who this Hubie is," Maxine said.

Ash eyed her. "He's a maintenance man. A good guy."

Estelle nudged her friend. "Can't be that good if the cops have him in handcuffs."

"Furthermore," Sylvia said to bring everyone's attention back to her, "I wouldn't murder a man for something I could take whenever I wanted."

"That's a good point," Maxine said. "If Sylvia

wanted, she could have taken it at any time. No need to harm anyone.”

“The manuscript was sent to the hotel,” Ash said. “Not to her. It was scheduled to be sold at the auction. She had to take it once it arrived here. She’d needed a plausible story to do so.”

“An ally, too,” Thelma said.

“If all of you are so smart,” Sylvia said, “search my room. You won’t find anything there.”

“That’s because it’s under his bed,” Thelma said with a prideful nod.

“What’s under whose bed?” Estelle asked.

“The manuscript. It was under Hercule’s bed in the basement.” Thelma made a motion like she was slipping something under a bed. Either that or she mimed like she was bowling. “I saw it.”

Estelle faced Thelma. “This one lives in a hotel basement, and you still want him to meet your daughter?”

“It’s only temporary,” Thelma said. “Hercule will get back on his feet soon enough.”

Ash waved his hand. They were getting off track, but he felt it necessary to say, “I’m not interested.”

Thelma appeared confused. “You said it wasn’t serious with the other woman.”

Estelle’s eyes slanted. “I bet he’s married, isn’t he?”

“I’m not married,” Ash protested. “There’s a woman I like.”

“Wait until you meet Kinsey,” Thelma said

proudly. "You'll change your mind."

Maxine disapprovingly shook her head. "A basement is no place to raise a cat."

Estelle clucked. "Pay attention, Maxie. Lots of things are happening."

"You're all missing the obvious," Sylvia said as she crossed her arms. "The maintenance man had access to the basement and a hammer. He stole the manuscript and put it under the bed. I'm innocent. End of story."

Maxine snapped her fingers. "If that's true, then the cops have solved it."

"We lost again." Estelle's shoulders slumped.

Ash shook his head. "Hubie didn't kill Ramon. He had no motive."

Thelma pointed to Sylvia. "So we're back to her and Nadine stealing the manuscript."

"I didn't steal anything," the conference president protested.

"You still could have killed Ramon," Thelma said.

"I had nothing to do with that, either."

Maxine cocked her head. "You called him a dirty dog, though."

"Sounds like you liked him," Estelle added.

Ash headed for the exit of the silent restaurant.

"Where are you going, Hercule?" Thelma asked.

"To get to the bottom of this."

Chapter 15

Ash didn't want to be in the north hallway again. It went against his self-preservation instincts. With so many cops running around the hotel, there were too many chances for Ash to get snared by one of them. He knew it was bound to happen, but he wanted to get as many questions answered before they caught him. Hopefully, he could solve the mysteries surrounding the day's events.

Right now, though, it didn't appear any law enforcement personnel were this far down the corridor. They must be clustered around the crime scene and in the lobby. Only hotel guests wandered in this section of the hotel, and none of them paid Ash any attention.

He hurried toward the door to the north stairwell.

Ash wanted to find Ramon's killer and get justice for his friend. If the cops found the murderer first, so be it. He wasn't looking for retribution.

He firmly believed Nadine stole the manuscript, and she planned to take it with Sylvia's help. Perhaps Ramon was in on the heist; perhaps he wasn't. The two women had conspired to take the manuscript. Ash was sure of it.

Why then did Sylvia seem surprised when she learned of Nadine's arrival at the hotel? Was Nadine planning a double-cross? Or had the hotel manager simply forgotten to alert Sylvia about her arrival at Coastal Haven?

Questions continued to plague Ash as he arrived at the stairwell door.

If Nadine took the manuscript before Ramon's murder, could the manuscript still be the motivation for that crime? What if the killer expected Ramon to have it? Perhaps Ramon found a buyer, then failed to deliver? If so, how did this buyer happen to have a hammer? Also, how had the manuscript ended up underneath Ash's bunk? He wasn't likely to get the truth from Nadine or Sylvia.

Ash grabbed the door's handle and took a final glance down the hallway. No cops wandered the concourse, but he noticed an attractive blonde woman in a red dress watching him.

He let go of the door handle and stepped toward her. Vivienne Hart turned and walked away, not bothering to look back. He wanted to ask how his likeness ended up on the cover of her novel. It had nothing to do with the task at hand and was likely a waste of time. Still, he watched her until she disappeared around the hallway bend, wondering how an artist picked his face and features from the ether.

Ash gently opened the stairwell door and stepped onto the first-floor landing. He paused long enough to listen for anyone moving on the steps. Hearing nothing, Ash let the door slowly close. He started up the stairs, two at a time.

Several other details troubled Ash. First, where had Hubie been since he supposedly fixed the leak in room 308? The man hadn't responded to repeated calls on the radio. He had never done that before and had even admonished Ash for not answering earlier in the day.

Next, who let Joey Marino into unit 308 after Ash ensured the room was locked? Since most of the hotel staff were out sick today, there were only a handful of options.

Ash reached the second-floor landing, grabbed the stairwell railing, and propelled himself up the next batch of stairs.

Perhaps Nadine let Marino into the room. The hotel manager had a master key, just like the maintenance men and the cleaning staff. The porters never got one. She knew who Marino was when Ash mentioned the bookie's enforcer but acted surprised that he was in the hotel. Perhaps Nadine planned to sell, trade, or give the rare manuscript to the thug for some reason.

However, Ash believed there weren't many readers in the criminal world. On the surface, it looked like guys read more while in prison. Ash knew this to be false. The most requested titles were reference books with lots of pictures. He didn't start reading until he arrived in Maine, under the guise of the Witness Protection Program, and he only did that to impress

Daphne Winterbourne.

If someone was going to buy the manuscript, they would do it for one of two reasons. They either deeply respected the author, or they believed they could sell the document for even more. Love or greed were almost always at the root of any crime.

Ash reached the third-floor landing. He noiselessly opened the door and peered into the hallway. No one was in the corridor. He stepped out and quietly closed the door behind him. He hadn't heard anyone else in the stairwell, but there was no need to take a chance.

Besides Nadine, Hubie had the ability to let Joey Marino into room 308. Ash thought it was a stretch, but it didn't make it wrong. Improbable was not impossible. Hubie surely seemed to be the guy who did what was right. He never gave off a vibe of being shady or questionable.

However, as the sole maintenance man working, he had the most access to tools. Hubie could have used a hammer to kill Ramon and still had an extra one to carry around. Perhaps he was the person in the basement that Officer Greenway heard. After killing Ramon, Hubie might have been down there getting a second hammer. That still didn't explain his disappearance for the past couple of hours.

Ash stopped in front of room 308. The door was slightly open. There were voices inside, low and unhurried. He couldn't make out what was being said, but it sounded like a man and a woman.

What kind of entry was best? Jump in fast and catch the room's occupants off-guard? Go in slow and perhaps overhear what the occupants were saying? In the end, the choice didn't matter.

The door to room 308 swung open, and Emily Larson hopped back, startled.

"What are you doing here?" Ash and the cleaning woman asked at the same time.

***

Not many things truly surprised Ash anymore. After a misspent youth followed by life as the Satan's Dawgs' bookkeeper, he experienced many circumstances that would shock a normal man. Dirty cops, rival gangs, and jealous boyfriends made for a violent life. Even though he was trying to walk the path of a better man, the last few months in the Witness Protection Program only added to his experience.

Seeing Emily in the doorway of room 308 confused Ash more than anything. His mind whirred for an explanation.

The cleaning woman's eyes were red, as if from crying. She put her hand on the door, a feeble attempt to block Ash from entering. "I'm cleaning," she said.

"You already cleaned it," Ash said. He'd smelled the cleaning products earlier when he first visited with Thelma Bennett.

"No, I didn't." Her voice wavered as she tried to be assertive, but her eyes betrayed her.

He looked over her shoulder. The broken lamp still lay on the floor, and the small desk sat cattywampus next to the wall—evidence of his fight with Joey Marino.

Ash glanced up and down the hallway to ensure he didn't miss something. "Where's your cart?"

"What's it matter?" she snapped. The confrontational attitude was unlike her. He'd only known her for a short time, and she'd always been quiet, almost mousey.

He leaned closer to the woman. "Is Marino still in there?" he whispered. He expected the bookie's thug to step around the corner and restart their earlier fight.

Emily's lips pinched together, and a tear ran down her cheek. "Who?"

"Joey," Ash said. "I heard voices."

She sniffled. "You heard wrong."

He put his hand on the door, towering over her. "Let me in, Emily. Please."

The cleaning woman stiffened. A scared puppy doing her best to seem brave. "You need to go."

Ash was about to insist on entering the room. If he had to, he'd gently push her out of the way. Something was going on inside the room, and he wanted to know what. Was Joey Marino still there? If so, had he threatened Emily into helping him? It's the only reason he could imagine Emily being so scared.

Her lower lip trembled, and tears welled in her eyes. It was then Ash realized he'd misread Emily's emotions. She wasn't scared; she was sad.

"He ain't going away," Joey Marino said from deeper in the room. "Let him in."

"What's going on?" Ash whispered.

Emily didn't answer. Instead, she pushed the door open and motioned for Ash to enter.

Three long strides and he was in the hotel room, staring at Marino. The enforcer sat upright on the bed. He held a bloody washcloth to his head.

"The porter," Joey said. "Coming back to finish the job?"

"He's the one who hit you?" Emily asked.

"I said he looked like a waiter." He waved a hand. "Not anymore, I guess. Nice tattoos."

It hit Ash then. Earlier in the day, Ramon had said his new girlfriend was perfect, except she had a thug for a brother. Ash hadn't put two and two together until right then.

"You're siblings," he said.

"Look at him." Joey laughed without mirth. "Using ten-dollar words. Got a dictionary in your pocket?"

Emily nodded. "He's my brother."

"How's that work?" Ash asked. "You're a Larson. He's a Marino."

"We grew up in a foster home," Emily said. "It wasn't a nice place, and Joey looked out for me."

Joey motioned toward his sister. "We looked out for each other. Like family."

Ash's eyes narrowed as he studied Emily. "You introduced Ramon to Joey."

"Yeah," Emily said, her eyes turning down. "Worst decision I ever made."

"Hey, oh," Marino said. "I'm sitting over here."

Emily's eyes cut to him. "I wish I'd kept you two apart."

"He was a grown man," Joey insisted. "He could bet if he wanted. Mr. Leo wasn't twisting his arm."

Emily bit her lip and looked toward the ceiling. "Mr. Leo wouldn't say no to anyone betting their last dollar."

"He's been good to me," Joey said.

Ash wanted to derail the sibling bickering. "Why are you crying?" he asked Emily.

Sadness returned to her face and her shoulders dipped. "Joey told me about Ramon."

"Just now?"

"A bit ago. When I returned to the room and found him on the floor."

Joey lifted his chin in Ash's direction. "Your friend did that."

Emily wiped at her tears. "I'm sure you deserved it."

"Watch it."

"Or what?" She smirked. "Big talker. You're not going to hit me, Joey. You know it."

"Eh." He flicked his hand in her direction. "Remind me never to loan you money."

"You don't. Mr. Leo does."

"You know what I mean."

Emily turned her attention back to Ash. "I ran

downstairs to check if it was true, if Ramon was really dead. That's when I saw all the cops."

"Why didn't you just call him on the radio?"

"Because he was dead," Joey said. "Are you thick?"

Emily waved off her brother. "Cleaning staff don't call the concierge. It's not done."

Ash didn't try to hide his confusion.

"Didn't you read the policy manual? Relationships between employees are forbidden. If we got caught, we both would have been fired. I need this job."

"It ain't that great," Joey said, lowering the bloody cloth from his head.

"I like it fine." Emily eyed her brother. "It's honest work."

"Suckers' work more likely."

"You loved Ramon," Ash said.

She brushed away more tears. "I'm not crying because I'm happy."

Ash's gaze shifted to Joey. It was even more unlikely the thug had killed Ramon. He claimed earlier it was better to have the man alive to pay back his debts, but would he really have harmed the man his sister loved? "You didn't kill him."

"That's what I said." Joey balled the bloody washcloth. "Are you slow?"

Emily glanced at her brother. "I would have killed him if he hurt Ramon."

Marino rolled his eyes. "Easy with the big talk."

"I'd do it," she said. "You know I would."

Ash asked, "Did Ramon hurt you?"

Emily slowly turned to him. "What're you talking about? Ramon never hit me."

Marino slipped one leg off the bed, his foot dropping heavily to the floor. "If he laid a hand on her—" He let the threat hang in the air.

There were several ways to hurt a man. Ash's former self specialized in the physical variety, but he knew a couple of women who perfected the other ways—emotional and mental. He avoided spending time with those ladies, preferring the hang-around girls who brought no drama to the mix. The short-term relationships might have been superficial, but he never worried about them twisting his thoughts.

Ash waved a hand. "Maybe he hurt you emotionally."

Emily's face pinched. "You saying he broke my heart?"

"He better not have," Marino said.

"He didn't." She looked at Ash. "What are you saying?"

Ash didn't know where he was going with the questions. It felt like he was running out of time. Very soon, his stay in Marlowe Bay would end. He needed to find Ramon's killer so he could have a couple of minutes with Daphne Winterbourne.

"Listen," Emily said, "I know the rumors about Ramon. The others whispered about it behind my back, but I heard them."

"What'd they say?" Ash asked.

"Stuff that wasn't true. Like Ramon was some sort of ladies' man. That he had flings with guests, even the celebrity ones. It was just jealous garbage. Understand?"

Ash stared at her as an earlier, interrupted thought again bubbled to the surface.

"You all right?" Marino asked. "Looks like you're about to have an aneurysm."

"Come down to the lobby," Ash said, backpedaling toward the door.

Emily followed him. "Why? What's going to happen there?"

"I think I've solved it."

"Ramon's murder?"

Ash didn't answer. He was too busy leaving the room. As he ran toward the elevators, he pulled his radio from his hip. "Hercule to Miss Marple. Are you there?"

A second later, Thelma Bennett responded. *"I'm here, Hercule. What's going on?"*

"Grab the Mavens and the Bookworms. I need your help."

Chapter 16

The elevator doors opened, and Ash stepped out. He walked confidently around the corner.

Guests filled the lobby, most of them watching the cops do their jobs. Officer Greenway stood with the handcuffed Hubert Dunn. The cop held a clear plastic bag with a hammer in it.

Another officer guarded the open storage room. Two more cops interviewed potential witnesses. Ash surmised other officers were likely still in the hotel. A couple might be around the corner at the murder scene, while more might be searching the hotel for him.

A woman in a business skirt stood next to a man in faded jeans and a T-shirt. The woman held a microphone by her side while the man rested a camera on his shoulder. Ash wondered if this was a local news crew or if it might have been Thelma's daughter, the reporter from Jacksonville. She was an attractive woman with the type of wholesome face local TV networks love, but the major networks seemed to avoid.

The Beautiful Bookworms and the Mystery Mavens were nowhere in sight.

Behind the check-in desk, Finley Hester leaned his elbows on the counter and held his chin in his hands. He seemed overwhelmed by the events occurring in the lobby right then. No guests waited to be processed.

A group of children ran around the fountain, dragging their hands in the water, and giggling as if the actions happening around them were everyday occurrences. Lorretta and Enoch Mayfield stood a few feet away and watched the kids with limited enthusiasm.

Nearby, Emily Larson and Joey Marino approached the lobby. Uncertainty filled their eyes.

In the middle of the lobby, Daphne and Carrie huddled together, watching the activity. Daphne glanced in Ash's direction, and they made eye contact. He smiled and waved, just a small little one, so he wouldn't call attention to himself.

"The porter!" Detective Landry yelled from the mouth of the north hallway. "Get him!"

"Detective," Ash called. "Can we talk?"

His request went unanswered as several of Marlowe Bay's finest ran toward Ash. Having been in this situation before, he lifted his hands in the air. "Easy, fellas. I give."

Perhaps they misunderstood Ash, or maybe he didn't speak loud enough to be heard over the drool-blowing cherub in the middle of the fountain. Whatever it was, two cops tackled Ash at full speed. A couple of linebackers wiping out a defenseless wide receiver standing on the sidelines.

Ash left his feet before landing squarely on his back. His breath escaped his lungs in a single whoosh of air.

"Stop resisting!" one cop yelled.

He wasn't.

"Stop fighting!" another shouted.

Again, he wasn't.

Ash lay as still as a dead fish. There was no reason to fight. He wanted to be in the lobby. Had this been during his days with the Dawgs, Ash surely would have fought. He might have landed a punch or two, but the cops always won in the end. They were the biggest gang, with the best weapons and training. It was never a fair fight.

The officers flipped Ash over to his stomach. In less than a couple of seconds, handcuffs secured his wrists. The cops jerked Ash to his feet and spun him around.

Landry stood nearby. Daphne and Carrie had moved closer as well. The reporter and cameraman lingered next to them. Ash lowered his head, trying to avoid looking directly into the lens.

"We found you," Landry said.

Ash stared at his shoes, not wanting to give the camera a better picture of himself.

"Look at me."

"Am I under arrest?" Ash turned slightly to show the handcuffs behind his back.

The detective grabbed Ash's chin and lifted his head. The cameraman crouched, likely getting a better shot.

"Right now," Landry said, "you're being detained until I figure out how you fit into this whole mess."

"I'm just a porter trying to do what's right."

"You're a pebble in my shoe." He thumbed over his shoulder at Officer Greenway. "Want to know what we found when we researched the records?"

"Not really."

"We found a fella out of Phoenix. A real hard case. His physical attributes match you right down to that fireball tattoo. What do you want to bet the rest of your tattoos match as well?"

"You're making a mistake," Ash said.

"That's what they all say."

A commotion erupted at the mouth of the north hallway. The Mystery Mavens arrived with Nadine Delacroix and Sylvia Grayson in tow. The group of women crossed the lobby until they were standing next to Ash and the detective.

"This is ridiculous," Nadine said.

"A miscarriage of justice," Sylvia added.

"Stow it, you two," Estelle said. She glanced around. "No Bookworms? I guess we win."

"I told you we would," Maxine said. "Didn't I tell you?"

Landry faced the Mavens. "What's this nonsense?"

Phyllis, the Maven with pink hair, pointed at Ash. "They arrested the porter!"

Maxine appeared confused. "Did he do it all along?"

Estelle clucked. "The joker fooled us, Maxie." She shook her head. "The wild goose chase was a hoax to get us out of the way."

"I told you," Nadine said. "I'm innocent."

Sylvia nodded at her friend. "We both are."

"What wild goose chase?" Landry asked.

"He asked us to corral these two," Estelle said, motioning to Nadine and Sylvia. "Guess it was so we couldn't win the competition."

The detective cocked his head. "What competition?"

"To solve the murder," Estelle said.

Maxine nodded. "It really felt like our year."

"I solve the murders," Landry said. He tapped himself on the chest. "Me." He glanced at Hubie. "I think the maintenance man did it."

"You do?" Maxine asked. She turned to Estelle. "We don't think he did it, do we?"

The leader of the Mavens put her hands on her hips. "What proof do you have?"

Landry pulled back, obviously offended by the question. "Not sure how that's any of your business."

The videographer pointed the camera lens at the detective and the reporter said, "Kinsey Bennett, Jacksonville 4 News. We'd like to know what proof you have, Detective."

Landry stared into the camera and stood straighter. A nervous smile spread across his lips. "Jacksonville, huh?"

"Yes, sir. Do you have a comment?"

"Well, it's like this," the detective said. "Maintenance men have access to the basement and the tools. They know their way around the stairwells. This one was the only one working today." The detective lifted two fingers. "Means and opportunity."

"What about motive?" Estelle asked.

"Motive is a luxury." Landry dismissively flicked his hand. "We don't need it to make an arrest."

The Mavens looked among themselves. "Books make it a big deal," Maxine said.

Ash jerked his head toward Nadine and Sylvia. "Those two stole the manuscript."

The videographer swung the camera around and Ash lowered his head.

"What was that?" Kinsey asked, extending a microphone. "What did you say?"

"All right," Detective Landry said, seemingly disappointed the camera was no longer on him. "Turn that off. I'll give you an interview in a moment."

"We have a right to be here," Kinsey protested.

"You can wait over there." Landry pointed toward the edge of the lobby. "Officers, escort the news team, please."

A couple of police officers walked the reporter and the videographer to the area the detective identified.

Landry crossed his arms and studied Ash. "What's this now about the stolen manuscript?"

The hotel manager and the conference president remained silent, but they exchanged worried glances.

Ash would have liked to motion to Sylvia, but his arms remained handcuffed behind his back. He jerked his head in her direction. "Sylvia lied when she told Officer Greenway the manuscript was worth ten thousand."

"That so?" Landry asked, glancing toward the conference president. "What's it really worth?"

"Ten times that."

The detective's eyebrows shot up.

"A hundred grand," Estelle chimed in.

Maxine nodded. "A hundred smackers."

Sylvia nervously chuckled. "I don't remember how much I said it was worth."

Ash continued. "She wouldn't secure it in the hotel safe but insisted it be kept in the concierge's storage room."

Landry's gaze bounced from Ash to Sylvia and back. "So Ramon was in on the heist?"

"What's with these guys and heists?" Nadine grumbled.

"Ramon wasn't part of the theft." Ash said, then looked at Joey Marino. "He had money troubles, but he didn't take it."

Landry followed Ash's gaze until it settled on the bookie's enforcer. "Look who it is. What are you doing here, Joseph?" He waved a hand at one officer standing behind Ash. "Put Knuckles over there in handcuffs until we figure out how he plays into this."

"Joey didn't kill Ramon," Ash said.

"You know this how?"

"Because I know who the killer is."

Detective Landry waved his hands. "Okay, okay. I think you need to start over."

Ash turned slightly. "I can share easier if these are off my wrists."

***

When Ash finished relaying what he knew about the manuscript theft, he looked toward Daphne and snuck a little wave, his hand never going above his waist. She smiled as their eyes lingered. Carrie Fenton nodded with approval. The Mystery Mavens nodded their approval at his story.

Detective Landry's nose crinkled. "The hotel manager and the conference president conspired to steal a hundred-thousand-dollar manuscript?"

"That's correct," Ash said.

"They certainly had the means and opportunity."

"Motive, too," Estelle added.

"Which supposedly is a luxury," Maxine said.

From the edge of the lobby, Kinsey Bennett held her microphone out. "Could you speak up? We didn't get the last part."

Frustration blossomed on Landry's face. He turned and motioned for everyone to move away. "Give us some room, people. Nothing to see here."

Several in the group groaned their displeasure as they shuffled back.

"After all the work we did," Maxine said.

Estelle smirked. "The detective's an ungrateful sort, isn't he? Makes the porter seem almost likeable."

Detective Landry frowned. "I'm not understanding why Nadine slipped the manuscript under the rollaway bed in the basement." He glanced at the hotel manager, then faced Ash again. "We could argue constructive possession if we wanted to put this at your feet."

Cops and prosecuting attorneys could argue for any fiction they wanted.

"Nadine came into the hotel to steal the manuscript," Ash said. "She'd been sick and wasn't supposed to be back. As soon as she had the manuscript, she ran downstairs and hid it in the first place she could find."

"Why not put it in her office?" Landry asked.

"Finley was acting as manager today. He had access to her office. Plus, she wasn't supposed to be in today. I was the only one besides Ramon who saw her."

The detective canted his head. "Why didn't she leave the hotel with it? Just jump in her car and go home."

"She couldn't leave," Ash said. "Sylvia had the contact who wanted the manuscript. Nadine wouldn't know who to sell it to."

Everyone looked at the conference president. "That's conjecture," Nadine said. "I don't know what he's talking about."

"Nadine knew about Joey Marino," Ash said, thumbing at the thug. "My guess is she knew about Ramon's gambling and was worried he might try to steal it before she had a chance."

Landry gnawed on his lower lip. "You said Sylvia didn't know Nadine took it at first."

"She didn't." Ash's gaze bounced between the

hotel manager and the conference president. "My guess? Sylvia revealed her crush on Ramon, which worried Nadine. Maybe she worried Sylvia would double-cross her to help Ramon."

Sylvia and Nadine exchanged unfriendly glances.

"Okay," Detective Landry said. "Maybe I'm buying some of this, but how'd the manager get the manuscript? What'd she tell Ramon?"

"She wouldn't have to tell him anything," Ash said. "She's the boss, right?"

Landry tapped a pen against the notepad for several seconds. Eventually, he said, "I guess that wraps things up."

Ash furrowed his brow. "It does?"

"Sure. The hotel manager and the conference president stole the manuscript. They asked the maintenance man to kill the concierge in the stairwell to keep him quiet about the heist, offering him a piece of the take."

Estelle shook her head as if clearing out a ringing in her ears. "That's a mouthful."

"Like a game of *Clue*," Maxine added.

Ash pointed at Hubie. "Was he found with a hammer?"

"He was," Landry said, "and I know where you're going with this. How could there be a hammer in the stairwell and one on his hip? He's a maintenance man. He had access to spare tools."

"I heard Greenway say there was no blood on the hammer in the stairwell."

Landry clicked his tongue against the back of

his teeth. "I've seen weirder things, and I'm sure the forensic types can explain it."

"When you caught Hubie," Ash asked, "what was he doing?"

Landry curled his lip. "Are you leading this investigation, or am I?"

"I was beginning to wonder," Estelle said.

Maxine leaned toward her friend. "The detectives on TV are always so handsome. This one, not so much."

"I don't know," Phyllis added from behind them. "I think the detective is rather distinguished."

Ash ignored the detective's challenging question and asked another. "Where did you find Hubie?"

"Not that it's any of your business," Landry said, "but he claimed he was at the hardware store, getting supplies."

Ash thought back to his conversation with Hubie. He had grumbled about being out of plumbing tape. Could he have gone to the store for that? Surely, that wouldn't have taken long.

"He had a receipt?" Ash asked.

Landry rested his hands on his hips. "What's with you? The man with the questionable background mucking around in my investigation."

"Trying to lend a hand." Ash smiled. "Like they do in the shows."

"We don't like amateurs sticking their noses where they don't belong."

Estelle barked a single, sharp laugh. "Oh,

boy. Get a load of that malarky. We helped him solve the manuscript theft, and he says he doesn't need us."

Maxine nodded. "What a load of hooey."

The detective glared at the Mavens, and the leaders of the group shuffled back, bumping into their other members.

"Was the receipt stamped?" Ash asked. "With a date and time?"

Landry spun toward him and stuck a finger in his nose. "Listen, you."

Ash lifted his hands in surrender. "I'm asking for a reason."

"Yeah? What reason?"

"Because Hubie Dunn isn't your murderer."

Detective Landry smirked. "Is that right, Sherlock? You going to tell me who is?"

A disturbance behind Ash caused him to look over his shoulder.

The Beautiful Bookworms entered the lobby with a cluster of conference attendees in their wake. At the front of the crowd was Thelma Bennett and an attractive blonde woman in a tight red dress. The art portfolio bag slung over her left shoulder.

Thelma waved at her daughter, who remained at the lobby's edge. Kinsey waved back with the microphone. Thelma motioned toward Ash with a questioning smile. Kinsey nodded approvingly.

"We'll get to the bottom of this now," Maxine said with a broadening smile. "Vivienne Hart is here."

Estelle clucked. "She hasn't worked this case one bit, Maxie. She won't know which way is up."

Thelma and Vivienne walked up to Ash and Detective Landry.

"Hello, Hercule."

"Miss Marple," Ash said.

Landry eyed Vivienne Hart. "You are?"

The author introduced herself with a fetching smile. She extended her hand and Landry reached for it.

"Careful, Detective," Ash said. "She murdered Ramon."

Chapter 17

The gathered crowd collectively inhaled at Ash's accusation.

"Not Vivienne." Maxine covered her mouth. "She wouldn't. She couldn't."

"Oh sure, she could," Estelle said. "Authors are sneaky sorts, sitting around all day thinking about murder."

Thelma shuffled back from Vivienne. "I could have been next."

Kinsey Bennett, Thelma's daughter, hurried closer with her microphone extended. "What a scene," Kinsey said to the videographer who sidled up next to her. He slowly swept the camera over the assembled guests. Ash didn't bother to hide his face now. It was too late.

Vivienne Hart put her hand on her chest. "I did what now?"

"You murdered Ramon," Ash said.

Detective Landry held up both hands. He said, "Everybody hold on now," but nobody listened.

Vivienne chuckled. "I'm a best-selling author."

"Which makes you a celebrity," Ash said, "I suppose."

Maxine pointed at Vivienne. "The most famous mystery romance author there is."

Estelle smirked. "I don't know about that."

"Ramon told me one of his girlfriends was famous."

"I'm his girlfriend," Emily Larson said, her eyes darkening. "His only girlfriend."

Maxine leaned toward Estelle. "What's happening? I'm lost."

Estelle motioned between Emily and Vivienne. "It's a love triangle."

"The concierge sure got a lot of action. Wonder what made him so special."

"Keep it clean, Maxie." Estelle shook her head in disappointment. "We're in public."

Maxine blushed.

Detective Landry raised his hands higher. "All right, all right. Enough. If you're not a porter or a best-selling author, I need you all to move toward the edge of the lobby."

Moans rose as everyone began to shuffle away. As the crowd disseminated, a hush descended over the lobby. Everyone wanted to hear what was about to be said.

Nadine Delacroix and Sylvia Grayson exchanged glances before heading in opposite directions.

"Except you two," Landry ordered. "Officers, grab those women and hold them until we sort everything out."

The officers who had tackled and roughly handcuffed Ash gently stopped the hotel manager and the conference president. They remained several feet away from Detective Landry.

Daphne Winterbourne stood on the south edge of the lobby. She craned her neck as if searching for something across the way. She abruptly scampered across the lobby. Carrie Fenton seemed surprised by this sudden action and hurried to keep up.

Landry shook his head at the two women and turned his attention back to Ash and Vivienne Hart.

"Now," he said. "Where were we?"

"I was being falsely accused of murder," Vivienne said. She pointed at the reporter and cameraman standing at the edge of the lobby. "Once this hits the airwaves, I'll have a publicity nightmare." Her finger swung toward Ash. "When that happens, I'm suing you for slander and taking you for everything you've got."

Ash shrugged. He didn't have much. A cat, a few previously read paperbacks, and a knitting kit were all he had to his name. The only article of value was Travis, and no court would take his cat as part of a settlement.

He continued, unafraid of the author's litigious threat. "The hammer found in the stairwell didn't have blood on it."

Vivienne crossed her arms. Her art portfolio was tucked underneath her left elbow. "Retract your accusation, sir, or you'll speak with my attorney."

"No blood on the hammer," Ash said, "means another murder weapon was used."

Detective Landry's eyes narrowed. "What other weapon are you proposing she used?"

"Check her bag."

Vivienne clutched the art portfolio to her chest. "You've got no right."

The detective thumbed over his shoulder. "The dead man in the stairwell says otherwise. Either you let me look, or we'll detain you long enough to get a warrant. End result is the same."

Vivienne's gaze swept over the lobby. Ash had seen that look before. She was looking for an escape route. There were none. Cops were everywhere, plus a reporter and cameraman documented her every action now. She was stuck.

Reluctantly, Vivienne pulled her portfolio from her shoulder and held it out for the detective.

Landry grabbed it and opened it. "What's this?" He pulled on a latex glove before lifting the square head magnifying glass from the bag. A large crack ran through the middle of the circular lens. "Heavy son of a gun," Landry said. He hefted it a couple of times. "Heavier than a small hammer."

"What's that made of?" Estelle called from the edge of the lobby.

"Brass, maybe," Thelma offered.

Landry inspected the magnifying glass closer. "What do we have here?" He motioned toward a corner of the square head. "Looks like blood and hair."

Vivienne pulled her shoulders back and thrust her chin out. "That was an illegal search and seizure." She pointed at the cameraman. "They saw it."

"Yes, they did," Landry said. "We'll make that exhibit A."

Vivienne Hart crossed her arms and set her jaw. "I want a lawyer."

"You'll get one, sister. Down at the station." Landry motioned for Greenway. "Arrest her."

Carrie Fenton reappeared at the north edge of the lobby. Right behind her was Daphne Winterbourne. She held Travis in her arms.

***

The Mystery Mavens and Beautiful Bookworms gathered around Daphne and Travis. They cooed over the cat. Thelma walked over to talk with her daughter.

"Look who we found," Daphne said smiling up at Ash.

"Hey buddy." Ash rubbed the cat's head smiling back at Daphne. The tom purred loudly in her arms and made no attempt to run away. The little traitor never did that with Ash.

"What's his name?" Phyllis, the pink-haired Maven, asked.

Ash said, "Travis," at the same time Daphne uttered, "Rhodenbarr."

Maxine cocked her head. "Travis Rhodenbarr?"

"No." Ash smiled. "Travis is my name for the cat." He pointed at himself, then motioned toward Daphne. "Rhodenbarr is her name for him.”

Estelle’s nose crinkled. “What kind of nonsense is this? You can’t have different names for a cat.”

“Sure you can,” Daphne said. “Whoever’s with the cat gets to name him.”

Carrie motioned to the cat. “I call him Sherlock.”

“Not very original for a writer,” Phyllis muttered.

Maxine blinked several times, obviously shocked at this revelation. “You must be joking. It’s disrespectful to treat a kitty this way.”

Ash continued to pet the tom. “Cats reflect the personality of whoever they’re with, so it’s natural we get to name them when we’re together.”

“It’s not natural,” Maxine said.

Estelle clucked. “It’s an abomination is what it is.”

“Tell them about the caveat,” Daphne said.

Ash nodded. “The only rule is the cat must be named after a mystery protagonist.”

Estelle scoffed. “Dumbest thing I’ve ever heard.”

“It borders on animal cruelty,” Maxine said.

A murmur of agreement ran through the assembled readers. Phyllis, however, appeared delighted. She announced, “I’m going to name him Ellery.”

Estelle spun and glared at her. “Stow it, Phyllis. If you go naming the cat, then everyone—”

Maxine's face suddenly brightened. "I'm naming him Nero, then."

"See what you started?" Estelle asked Phyllis.

Several of the gathered Mavens and Bookworms chimed in with their names of choice. They laughed among themselves at their various selections.

"The cat's going to have a complex now," Estelle grumbled. She turned back to Ash, Daphne, and the cat. Her lip curled in disgust before she shrugged a single shoulder. "Easy."

"Easy?" Ash asked.

"Easy Rawlins," Estelle said. "Walter Mosley's detective. That's my name for the cat."

"Something is still bothering me," Maxine said. "How'd you end up on Vivienne's book cover?"

"You're on a book cover?" Daphne asked.

Ash shrugged. "I'm not, but there's a strong resemblance."

"I bet it's AI," Estelle said. "Artificial intelligence is going to ruin everything."

The assembled mystery fans murmured their agreement.

Maxine eyed her friend. "So, what do you think?"

"About?" Estelle said.

"The conference. It's starting off pretty good."

Estelle smiled. "You know, Maxie, if the rest of the event goes the way it did today, it might be the best conference ever."

Maxine laughed. "You say that every year."

"C'mon," Estelle said. "Let's eavesdrop on the

cops." She waved for the Mavens to follow her. Even the Bookworms tagged along.

"We're finally alone," Ash said, smiling at Daphne.

Carrie rolled her eyes. "I'll take that as my cue to leave." She headed toward the fountain.

Daphne shook her head. "I still can't believe it's you. Have you been here since you left Maine?"

"No," he said. "I've bounced around. Only been here a short time."

Daphne considered the cat for a moment, then looked up. Her eyes softened. "You know."

She packed a lot of truth into those two words. Truth that Ash had felt since they kissed. "Yeah," he said. "I know."

Her eyes widened, and she leaned forward. The cat was between them, but Ash leaned down to kiss her.

"Is this the girlfriend you told me about?" Thelma Bennett asked. Her daughter, Kinsey, was on her heels. The cameraman stood a respectful distance away.

Ash straightened and his cheeks warmed. Was he blushing? He never blushed.

"Girlfriend?" Daphne asked. Confusion filled her eyes. "You have a girlfriend?"

"No," Ash said. "I don't."

Thelma beamed and pulled her daughter forward. "In that case, this is my daughter, Kinsey."

"Mom," Kinsey said with exasperation. "No."

Ash lightly touched Daphne's arm. "I said

there's a girl I like, Thelma."

The Beautiful Bookworm said, "This is the one?"

He nodded. "Yeah."

Daphne looked down, obviously embarrassed by his admission.

"Mind if we interview you?" Kinsey asked. She motioned toward the cameraman. "Vivienne Hart's arrest will make a much better story for our station than the conference."

"I'm sorry," Ash said. "I can't."

"Please, Hercule," Thelma said. "Do it for me."

He didn't want to disappoint the woman, but Ash also didn't want his face fully on any station, even if it was only one in Jacksonville. If he'd learned anything in his time in the Witness Protection Program, it was that nothing stayed local for long. So, he relied on an excuse that had gotten him out of trouble in the past. "Store policy."

"Huh?" Kinsey asked.

"Only the manager can talk with the press."

"She's been arrested," the reporter said.

Ash pointed at Finley Hester. "The desk clerk's in charge now. Interview him."

Kinsey exchanged glances with her mom. "I guess I'll go over there."

Thelma nodded. "I'll be along in a moment." She turned back to Ash. "Thank you for an exciting day. I hope I'll get to see you more this weekend."

He wasn't sure that would happen, but he smiled, nonetheless. "Me, too."

"Find me later," Thelma said, "and we'll look for that Chandler book." She wandered toward the front desk, where her daughter was now talking with Finley.

"Where were we?" Ash asked, knowing full well he was about to kiss her.

Daphne suddenly seemed embarrassed, and she looked down at the cat. "What book was she talking about?"

He shrugged. "I don't know. She said the Chandler fellow wrote some classics and I should read him."

"What're you reading now?" Daphne asked.

It seemed an odd subject to bring up, especially now. However, they had first met in a mystery bookstore, and they were at a mystery conference.

"Ever read Parker?" Ash asked.

"A few."

"I'm reading *Slayground* now."

She squinted. "Is that the one where the mob attacks Parker while he's hiding in the amusement park? Sort of unbelievable, don't you think?"

Ash shrugged. "Seems pretty believable to me."

Daphne lowered her head. "Did you really say that about me? That you like me?"

"More than like," Ash said. "I haven't stopped thinking about you since Maine."

"Ditto."

Ash leaned down to kiss her. Daphne closed her eyes and parted her lips just slightly.

A commotion in the lobby caused Ash to look up. Bodies shuffled out of the way and voices raised. Five men in jeans, boots, and blue windbreakers fanned out. Each held a sheet of paper in their hand as their eyes scanned those assembled. One man turned to speak with Detective Landry. On the back of his lightweight jacket were the words *U.S. Marshal.*

Ash turned to Daphne. "I have to go."

"When will I see you again?"

He shook his head. "It's not safe."

"You can call. Or write."

"It'll put you in danger," he said.

Daphne pulled her shoulders back and thrust out her chin. "I'm not afraid of danger."

Heavy footsteps headed his way. Ash didn't need to turn to know the marshals were coming over.

"I'll never stop thinking about you," Ash said.

"This isn't how our story is supposed to end."

"Yeah?" He smiled. "How's it supposed to end?"

Before she could answer, a deep male voice said, "Asher Reed, you need to come with us." A hand tightened around his elbow. "Now."

Ash glanced over his shoulder. The five marshals stood there now. The nearest one, the one with his hand clamped around Ash's elbow, made eye contact with him. The others scanned the room, ensuring no one would get any closer.

He turned back to Daphne. "I'm sorry."

"I understand." She handed Travis to him, and the tom stopped purring. "We never got our kiss."

He bent and she stood on her tiptoes. Their lips barely touched when the marshal tugged on him, pulling them apart. Still, Beau tingled inside.

"Mr. Reed," the lawman said, "we need to go now."

"Daphne," he said as she reached for him.

Ash backpedaled as the marshal pulled him from the lobby into the Marlowe Bay evening. Everyone turned in his direction, including the Mystery Mavens and Beautiful Bookworms. Some raised their cell phones to take pictures or videos.

The Jackson 4 News camera recorded the entire event.

Beau Smith
returns in…

Cozy Up
to Mayhem

About the Author

Besides writing the Cozy Up Series, Colin Conway is the author of the 509 Crime Stories, a series of novels set in Eastern Washington with revolving lead characters. They are standalone tales and can be read in any order.

Colin is also the co-author of the Charlie-316 series. The first book in the series, *Charlie-316*, is a political/crime thriller and has been described as "riveting and compulsively readable," "the real deal," and "the ultimate ride-along."

He served in the U.S. Army and later was an officer of the Spokane Police Department. He has owned a laundromat, invested in a bar, and run a karate school. Besides writing crime fiction, he is a commercial real estate broker.

Colin lives with his beautiful girlfriend, three wonderful children, and a codependent Vizsla that rules their world.

Learn more at colinconway.com.